READ

MY

SHORTS

Darcy Nybo

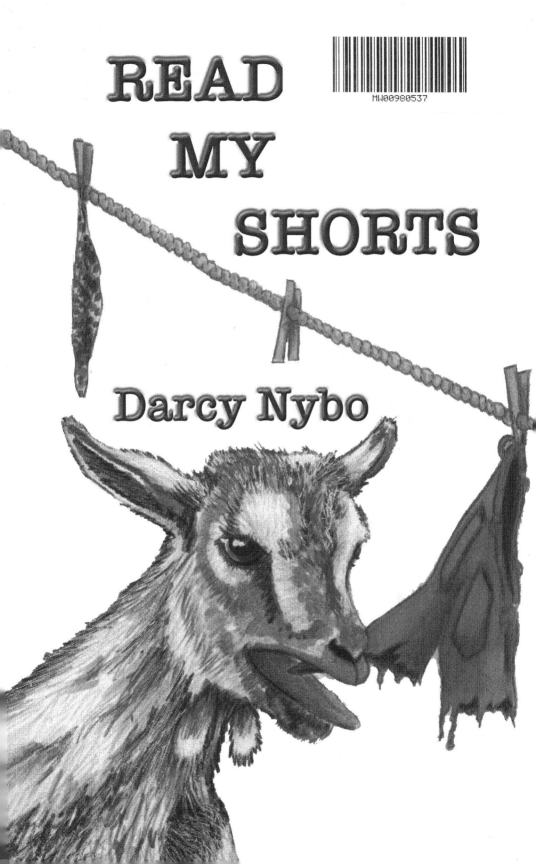

Ordering Information

Special discounts are available on quantity purchases by libraries, schools, corporations, associations, and others. For details, contact the author at darcy@alwayswrite.ca. Single books can be purchased on Amazon.

ISBNs

978-1-987982-03-9 (paperback)

978-1-987982-10-7 (eBook)

Disclaimer

All stories contained herein are works of fiction. Names, characters, businesses, places, events and incidents are either the products of the author's imagination or used in a fictitious manner. Any resemblance to actual persons, living or dead, or actual events is purely coincidental.

Cover created by Sharlene McNeill

Published with Artistic Warrior Publishing

artisticwarrior.com

Read My Shorts

Kathleen
Enjoy!
Darcy Nybo

This book is dedicated to every single one of our essential workers who helped us through the COVID-19 outbreak. I thank you from the bottom of my heart.
You are our heroes.

Darcy Nybo

ABOUT THE STORIES

Some of these stories were written for contests, some were winners, some came in second and third, and others didn't make the cut. Others I wrote because the idea was there and needed to come out. No matter how they were conceived, they are here now for your reading enjoyment.

Sci-Fi and Fantasy

Sarah, 1489: A story set in the not so far future. Frozen people, a cruise ship, and young love combine in this sci-fi short with a chilling ending.

Even a Goddess Needs a Break: Being queen of the underworld is not an easy task. Every now and then, even a goddess needs a break.

Ten Percent: Aliens, the end of the world, and vanity. Find out what happens when you make yourself into something you're not.

Ghost Stories

The Crutch: Jeremy has been stricken with panic attacks since adolescence. Now middle aged, he finds a crutch from his past near a dumpster behind Tim Hortons. The end result is rather shattering.

The Utah Den: Rosemary does not handle change well, so when the hotel's busy season forced her into sharing a room with a strange man, she was quite perplexed. In the end, being alone with a dark handsome stranger benefited everyone. Hint: Utah Den is an anagram for Haunted.

The Will: Felicity Rathbone crashes a dinner party to speak to a psychic about her deceased husband's Will. What she finds out, will change her forever.

Mystery
Murder in the Cards: Poker players are dying and Detective Jacoby, with a little help from a rookie cop, may be able to figure out who did it and why.

Secret Chef: Ash McKenzie desperately needs to win a contest put on by her culinary school. Will falling asleep cost her the prize, or make her the star of the show?

Action/Adventure
Survivor: A chilling dash for freedom with a bloody exciting ending!

Pooper Scooper: Gordon hates his life as dog walking, pooper scooper. Then a black cat crosses his path, changing his life forever.

The Last Jump: The worst distance between two people is miscommunication. Especially at 5,500 feet when someone is about to jump.

Reap What You Sew: Sometimes it's not always business as usual, especially when it comes to this particular tailor.

Inline Shopping: An innocent trip to the grocery store escalates into quite the fracas.

Romance
Mabel's Gentleman Caller: It's the early 1900s and Mabel is afraid she'll become an old maid. Then she meets Gus, and her world is shaken in more ways than one.

Darcy Nybo

The Test: A chance meeting reunites fledgling lovers. Will they survive the test?

Fairy Tales

BB and the Pig: Stanley the pig was homeless because of a selfish, mean wolf. One day, after a chance encounter with the same wolf, he makes a wish that could change his life for the better, if he believes in himself.

Janai's Wishes: Janai is tired of being short and ignored by her parents. She meets the oddest fairies who grant her wishes. However, those wishes have consequences.

General Fiction

Deer God: A missing plane, a wounded deer, and one woman's battle making sense of it all.

Half A Man: George had a stroke and now feels like he's half a man. Why can't his family see how much things have changed?

Her Breasts: One man, one woman, decades together, and one constant: her breasts.

Micro Fiction – the shortest of the shorts

Fore for Four: Sometimes a round of golf is not what it seems.

The Secret Hallway: A very short love story.

Grandpa's Other Name: What's in a name?

SCIENCE FICTION/FANTASY

GHOST STORIES

MYSTERY

ACTION/ADVENTURE

GENERAL FICTION

ROMANCE

FAIRY TALES

MICRO FICTION

Sarah, 1489

Devlin keyed in the 10-digit security code for the cruise ship elevator. He'd copied it from his mother's notebook in their stateroom. The elevator was near the engine room in a restricted area and he wasn't supposed to be there. He didn't care. He didn't want to be on a stupid cruise ship with his stupid mother. He was twelve and wanted to be at the virtual reality decks with his friends. Devlin was travelling with his mother because his father was away on business and apparently they thought he wasn't old enough to stay home alone. It was all crap as far as Devlin was concerned. He was plenty old enough. Sure, it was cool that his mother was part of a team transporting frozen people to be thawed out, but taking five days to get there was a bore. They were going to Great Yarmouth, Europe's newest medical mecca. There was no one his age on board, only millennials trying to recapture their youth. That and a few white coats who guarded the pod people.

The elevator stopped deep in the belly of the ship. When the doors opened, Devlin was assaulted by a smell that left a metallic taste in his mouth. His eyes adjusted to the blue light as he made his way to a room near the back. Four days ago he'd discovered where the *not so alive* passengers were stored and one of them fascinated him.

Devlin keyed in another code and the thick glass doors slid open. He made his way over to, Sarah, number 1489. His stomach fluttered as he removed the ePad from the container's metal pocket. He took a deep breath and turned it on. The screen lit up and shared its secrets. Sarah Jennings. Age fourteen. Airborne contagion X45Z3. He stared at her photo. She was so beautiful. Her eyes captivated him. He'd fallen in love with a girl he'd never met. He wanted to kiss her.

The ePad contained Sarah's doctor's notes and a short diary of her days before being placed in a cryonic coma. Devlin had been reading the notes and her diary for four days now. He scrolled down to the last entry.

April 15, 2020
Dear Diary:
I had the dream again last night. The nurse woke me just as we were kissing. I can still feel his arms around me, the way his brown eyes looked into my soul, and the taste of his lips. I told her about the dream once. She said it was the fever. I know he's out there. I can feel it. All my family and friends will be gone when I wake up, but he will be there. I know it with all my heart. They're doing the procedure in an hour. I'm scared, but I'm so tired of the way people look at me. Some of my friends died from

this sickness. The rest aren't allowed to see me. I haven't seen my mother's smile in over a month because she has to wear a mask when she visits. Her eyes are always red and puffy. My father won't visit any more. He says he can't take the chance. It doesn't matter, though, my love will be there when I wake up. I know it. I can hardly wait to kiss him for real and start my new life. I'll be like Sleeping Beauty, awakened by true love's kiss.

Devlin tapped the ePad and her photo appeared again. He knew she'd been dreaming of him. Sure, he hadn't even been born yet, but he knew. He was a miracle baby; one of the first conceived and born of an artificial womb. This was his destiny. He put the ePad to his lips and kissed Sarah's photo.

Someone was coming so he slipped the ePad back into its metal pocket and crouched behind the pod.

"This lot goes first." Devlin recognized his mother's voice. "1475 to 1500. It's a pity we have to destroy them, but they've passed their fifty-year expiry date."

Destroyed? No, that couldn't be true. These pods were going to Great Yarmouth to be unfrozen, revitalized, brought back. They couldn't destroy his Sarah.

The workers left to get the transport container and Devlin's mother left to finish her paperwork. He searched the room for something, anything he could use to open the metal pod, but found nothing. He went back to Sarah and ran his hands over the cylinder. The second time around he felt a slight indent in the metal. He touched it gently, heard a click, and flipped open the cover to expose an alphanumeric keypad. It wasn't hard to figure out. He typed in 1489X45Z304152017 and it worked. Her pod number, her illness code and the date she was frozen. Easy peasy. There was a hiss as oxygen flowed into her chamber. A few minutes later the pod opened. Devlin stepped back. This girl had ghastly white skin and sunken cheeks. Her lips were scabbed and her body was skin and bones. A monitor lit up and showed a faint heartbeat. It was now or never. He leaned in and placed a light kiss on her cracked lips.

"No!" his mother shouted from beyond the glass door. She looked straight at Devlin and began to cry. She pressed a button and her voice boomed through the loudspeakers. "Code 47." She took a deep breath, opened a panel, and pressed a button. "Decontamination protocol engaged."

She pressed an intercom button and Devlin heard her sobbing. "Oh Devlin, what have you done? I'm so sorry." He watched her press another button and felt the temperature in the room drop. "It'll only take a minute honey. I love you so much."

"Sorry for what, Mom?" He was confused and cold.

He looked over at Sarah. Her eyes fluttered open and she smiled. The last thing he heard was, "I knew you were real."

Even A Goddess Needs a Break

A gull screeched in protest as it watched a wave collapse on shore atop its would-be lunch. The sand crab washed back out into the ocean as the wave retreated. A lone figure laughed at the bird, waved its arm and the small sand crab appeared back on the beach. The gull greedily snatched it in its beak and carried it off over the waves.

The figure was dressed in a simple brown tunic and leggings. As it drew near, it became apparent it was female. Her long, dark-brown hair cascaded across her shoulders and flowed down her back. Her legs were strong and shapely and the swell of her breasts were visible beneath her loose tunic. There was a twinkle in her eye that was discernible from a distance, though none were near to see it. There was also a weariness, an almost imperceptible sadness beneath the surface, hidden by her quick step and smiling face. She looked like an amazon warrior of days gone by, perhaps on a much-needed leave, and indeed she was, on leave.

Her name was Ansuz. In the long-forgotten past, she was known by other names. None of those mattered today. She walked away from the ocean and found a spot to sit. She removed her boots and leggings and put them in her pack. She closed her eyes, sighed, and ran her toes through the sand.

Her work was so demanding. Although she was rarely

alone, she found herself to be lonely at times. She smiled as she remembered days from long ago—carefree days when she was but a child.

She lay back on the sand, closed her eyes and recalled her youth. The Great Halls were hers to romp and play in. She thought her life was normal then. Her father, the handsome giant Loki and her mother, the hideous Angraboda, gave her free reign of their lands. She had two older brothers, one a snake and the other a hell hound. She knew her birth mother was not her father's wife, but that was how things were when you were a high-level god. His wife, Sigyn, adored her father. None of this was unusual to her. They were her family. She was raised amongst the gods and goddesses of an era when Valhalla reigned supreme. At the time of her birth she was named Hela, Hel for short.

She remembered sneaking into Valhalla to see the great Odin. She did so by disguising herself as one of his own. It was then she chose the name Ansuz. She loved Odin dearly and enjoyed watching him tending to his warriors, training them and healing them. Many a great feast was held in their honour.

Ansuz opened her eyes and smiled. A soft breeze raised the hair on the back of her neck. It felt cool to her, cool and alive. She scanned the horizon and pushed her toes deeper into the sand. She watched them as they wiggled deeper and deeper until only her ankles were visible. She sighed again as she recalled the joyous celebrations at Valhalla. She missed watching the brave warriors roam the halls after battle. They sang songs of conquests and praised the battle that caused their death. They praised Odin and as they sang, all their wounds were healed. It was such a contrast to the realm where Ansuz now served as queen. It had been aeons since the sending, since the day she was deemed a monster. Odin had decreed it and she was cast into Niffleheim and given the task to rule over the underworld.

Ansuz shook her head, stood and stretched. She slowly pulled her feet out of the cool sand and dusted off her behind. Perhaps a swim would help relax her. She left her pack behind and sauntered towards the shoreline as if she were a young girl without a care in the world. A slight frown crossed her face. While hers was not a pleasant task, it was also not unpleasant. Her home, her queendom, was the way station, the jumping off point, for those who died and not been lucky enough to be accepted as warriors. She had her own Grand Hall that she called Elvidner. It was not as grand as the Grand Hall of Valhalla, but it was hers.

She and Odin were more alike than not. They had their positions, above and below. She fed lost souls, poor wandering creatures, at her table of Hunger. She divvied up her meagre supply of food with her knife of Starvation. She was not alone in her tasks. She had her maid, Agony and her manservant, Delay. They assisted her tirelessly with her daily duties in the underworld. They were never seen to move, yet they went about their duties with efficiency.

Ansuz decided to change the name of her domain to Hel after numerous failed attempts to get the newly dead to pronounce Niffleheim. It was bad enough that most could not assimilate the fact of their death, let alone trying to explain where they were.

All in all, life was good for Ansuz, considering her role in the grand scheme of things. When she was lonely, she had her loyal, bloodstained dog, Garm, to keep her company. He guarded the gates of Hel and ensured only the souls of the dead enter. At night, he took his place at the foot of her bed of Care.

Hel was not a dull place since Ansuz took over—far from it. When she was bored, she decorated her realm with the Glimmering Misfortunes of others. Some souls found her frightening, others found her comforting, and all found her to be quite odd. All could agree that she was a charming hostess.

It was time to relax now. A mini-vacation from Hel; a place she had lived and ruled for countless centuries. Today was time for a much-needed rest. It was a time to explore the world where souls come from.

There had been so much written about her, about her duties, her place, and so much of it was written wrong. But that was not hers to change. Ansuz stared at her toes and drew crude drawings in the sand with her foot. She took a few more steps towards the ocean and stopped at the water's edge. Hands on the small of her back, she stretched her entire body and raised her face to the sky. Then she slowly lowered her head and looked out over the cool, inviting ocean.

Yes, she was the Queen of the dead, ruler of ice and snow and eternal flame. But she was not the horrible monster the writers of history have portrayed her as. Those writers were, like many of that time, "Men!" she hollered out at the ocean. "Can't get nuthin' straight."

Ansuz looked back to her pack, raised her hand, snapped her fingers, and the pack appeared beside her. She reached inside and grabbed a piece of shrivelled meat and slowly chewed on it. She thought about the ocean and wondered of the secrets it held in its depths. She loved the smell of the ocean. It smelled of life and the freshness and unbridled energy that came from the living. She loved the feel of the spray, the warmth of the sun, the freshness of the air. There were bodies of water in her realm, but they were stagnant, putrid things. They ate the memories of souls until they were picked clean making the souls ready to be sent onwards to their final destination.

Ansuz swallowed her last bit of meat and gazed out to the reef. A large sailing ship rounded the corner of the bay. She heard shouts of rebellion and anger carried to her by the winds.

She sniffed the air. The smell of death was weak but growing strong.

"Damn it!" she cried as she kicked the sand. "I finally get a day off and it looks like it's going to be a very busy day in Hel." She thought a moment and decided it was Agony and Delay who would be the busy ones. After all, it was her day off. She trusted them and knew they would keep the souls safe until her return.

She picked up her pack, slung it over her shoulders, and closed her eyes. Her body shimmered and disappeared from the beach. Seconds later she appeared before Agony and Delay. She handed them her pack and informed them of the impending deaths on the ship. She gave instructions to insure all was ready for their new arrivals. The souls would be in good hands, as she had some relaxation and a bit of mischief to tend to. In a scant space of time she was back once again on the beach. The ship was closer now and the shouting was louder, angrier. She waded into the water, then dove beneath the waves and swam towards the ship. This would be fun. The opportunity to do mischief always raised her spirits. She was more her father's daughter than she chose to believe.

Her father, the great Loki, the trickster. How handsome he had been! Sigyn, his dear wife, always accepted him and his crafty ways. Even fathering children with another woman, didn't faze her. Sigyn stayed with him. Such were his ways with women, handsome and devilish in his humour, he captured their hearts and their minds. Ansuz had inherited much of his charm and love of mischief.

Ansuz glided smoothly towards to bow of the ship. She found a rope ladder and silently pulled herself up on deck. She could have just appeared there, but she'd save the theatrics for later. Men were screaming obscenities which could be heard above the clash of metal on metal. A deep, gruff voice cried out at the bow of the ship. Ansuz watched the lumbering red-headed man as he dodged the flying tankards and bottles thrown at him. A dodge, a duck, a sidestep, it was like a dance as he avoided the hurled objects while fending off a trio of armed swordsmen with his own sword. She perched atop a large crate and watched the melee with glee.

"I'm your captain! You can't take my ship away from me!" Spittle glistened on his beard as he thrust forward, skewering one of his attackers on his long sword. He placed a heavy foot on the now dead man's chest and pulled his blade free just in time to fend off another blow.

"It's mine I tell ya! It's mine! Back away now, or I'll have all yer heads on a platter! All of them, you hear!" The captain spun on his heels and found himself face to face with Ansuz. Shock and surprise flooded his face. She waggled her fingers at him in a friendly wave. Caught off guard, a tankard caught him squarely in the jaw. He stumbled and fell into the netting. His sword flailed wildly as his attackers lunged at him, piercing his flesh with their swords, spitting and screaming obscenities, swearing vengeance on mothers, fathers, sisters, and brothers.

Ansuz watched from her perch as the man was finally overcome. The angry mob lifted him easily over their heads, heedless of the droplets of blood that dripped from his body onto their hands, faces, and clothing. With a great cry of victory, they heaved the pirate captain overboard and cheered as his body hit the waves and slowly sank beneath the surface.

Ansuz stood and clapped loudly. "Such a fine performance. Such grace. Such style." She jumped off a crate and landed in front of who she presumed to be their new leader.

"All of you against one lone man. My, what brave lads you are!" The elder of the men began to speak, but Ansuz raised her hand to stop him.

"You have no honour, sir, do not speak to me. Any group of wild dogs can attack their leader when provoked. That still doesn't make them any more than dogs." Ansuz bowed deeply and made her way to the side of the ship. She stopped and turned towards the group; bloodlust still evident in their eyes.

"I presume you did this for vengeance and no doubt

that crate of treasure over there." Ansuz lifted her right arm and began to make swirling motions in the air. The top of the crate flew off, hitting a man in the back, sending him sprawling to the deck.

"Ah, greed. Such a fine thing, is it not!" Ansuz held out her hand as if beckoning to the treasures within the crate. One by one they floated upwards until they hovered high above the amazed group of mutineers.

"Well, greed shall be your downfall then." Ansuz winked at a man who was slowly inching towards her. He stopped, looked puzzled, and then followed Ansuz's gaze above his head. The last thing he saw was a solid gold bust as it smashed into his skull.

"That's one!" Ansuz clapped her hands gleefully as the multitude of riches rained down upon the heads and bodies below. She watched as one by one they were felled by heavy golden and silver treasures. Gold chains and strings of pearls sprang to life and strangled sea worn necks, crucifixes lodged into ears and eyes, gold coins lodged in throats, a jewel encrusted sword pierced the man who had orchestrated the coup d'état.

A few minutes later the deck was quiet. The wind gently tugged at the sails as the boat rocked back and forth. It would have been soothing if not for the scene on deck. Every now and then a moan sprang from the lips of a soul begging for release. Ansuz made her way across the deck, tapping her once sand-covered toes into the thigh, shoulder, or chest of a dying man. Each tap sent the souls rushing towards her kingdom.

"I shall see you all in Hel," she said as she poked the last body with her big toe. "But not just yet," she added. "I still need a relaxing swim."

Ansuz dove off the boat and followed wisps of blood downwards towards the unfortunate pirate captain. She slowed as she reached his body and watched with fascination as his blood swayed gently around him. The sharks would come soon and there would nothing left but the soul. It was a nasty way to go, but such was the fate of lawless men. At least this one was already dead.

She reached out to touch the gently swaying mop of red hair as it floated above him. Much to her surprise he opened his eyes and grabbed her wrist. His face was a portrait of pain, anger and confusion. She smiled at him and easily pulled away.

"Help me." He mouthed into the darkening water.

Ansuz pondered this for a moment. She watched as the last bit of air escaped his lungs. She glanced upwards as a great white shark passed overhead. She looked back to the man and thought thoughts only the goddess of Hel would think. She gave her shoulders a small shrug, then enclosed the man in a gentle embrace.

Her form shimmered as the darkness enveloped them

both. She waved to the shark as it advanced on its prey. The shark picked up speed, intent on its meal. Mouth open wide, the killing machine closed in and then chomped down into nothingness. It thrashed back and forth, searching for its prey. There was none.

Only a gentle laugh was left behind in the gloom. Her break was over.

Ten Percent

Hazel stood when her name was called. It was eerie, being here with these strange creatures. It was as if her life prior to this moment no longer had any real meaning, and her future was all she could think about. She squeezed her husband's hand once, let go, smiled, and stepped up to wait in her line.

She looked around. Her husband Steve gave a thumbs-up as she glanced his way. There was so much to take in. There were seven lines in all. She recognized people from her neighbourhood in some lines. The newspapers said this was happening everywhere. Every town and city in every country in every part of the globe had stations like this set up. People were being processed. The creatures were taking them home.

As she looked around, she realized for the first time in years; she wasn't cold. It had been freezing lately. Hazel smiled when she thought about going home. When she was younger, she had fantasized about being taken away on a huge spaceship. She belonged with the people from the stars; she knew it, and now it was happening.

A lady in the line to her left stepped into a clear plastic tube structure. A clear door closed, and a glowing purple light filled the tube. The woman inside smiled and closed her eyes. Hazel turned away, ashamed to be watching what appeared to be a very private moment. She heard a whoosh and turned to watch the woman step out through the back of the tube. A slender creature put his arm around her shoulder and led her to a red door. The woman stepped through and the door closed. The creature took his position again at the exit for the tube.

Hazel counted seven tubes, one for each line. She felt a tap on her shoulder. She turned and saw Steve in a line beside her. She hadn't even heard his name called.

"Hey hun, looks like we get to go through at the same time." Steve beamed at her.

Hazel smiled back. "Looks like it. This place is amazing, isn't it?"

Steve nodded and looked around the room. Hazel couldn't help but admire her husband's profile. His chin was strong and square, the cleft perfectly centred. His eyes were just the right distance apart and the most exquisite shade of blue. He smiled. That smile was worth every penny. It had cost $30,000: twenty-four teeth at $1,250 a tooth. They had opted to leave the back teeth alone and spend $5,000 for the chin and its cleft. They would have had the money for the back teeth the following year, but Steve's surgeon insisted his eyes could be the focal point of his face. All Steve had to do was forgo their Bahamas holiday and pay the surgeon their vacation money to fix his droopy lids.

Hazel rubbed a small scar on her cheek. It had been

over 20 years since the dog had attacked her. It left her with a thin white scar running from the bridge of her nose, across her cheek and under her ear. Steve said it didn't really show. Besides, you could cover a scar with make-up, but you couldn't un-droop an eyelid, square a jaw or make a perfect smile with cover up from the local drugstore.

Hazel realized it would be her turn soon. The soft whoosh of the tubes was getting louder. A buxom young blonde in front of her took a deep breath and stepped into the tube. Hazel looked away, curious, but not wanting to watch.

She turned towards Steve and reached across the gap between them to hold his hand. "We're up next." Steve winked at her and turned to watch the old man in front of him. "Geeze, would you look at the wear and tear on that one." Steve took his hand from hers and jerked his head towards the man entering the tube. "Just shoot me if I ever look like that."

The old man shuffled into the tube and stopped. Light showered down upon him. He closed his eyes. This time Hazel did not look away. She watched as his body appeared to straighten, as if the weight of his years were being lifted off. She continued to watch as the exit door opened. One of the slender creatures put an arm around the old man and led him to a red door. The blonde exited the tube in front of Hazel and was led through the green door.

It was time. Hazel and Steve stepped into their respective tubes. She hoped Steve would be okay. He'd been in a skiing accident a few years ago, a broken leg. While he was in hospital, he'd asked the doctors to do a pectoral implant on him. Steve left the hospital with a straight leg and perfect pecs. She stared down at her own imperfect breasts. Her left one sagged a little, the right pointed to the right instead of straight ahead. Steve said it didn't matter.

Between her job as a nurse and his job in sales, they could afford some nice things. Steve invested most of their money into himself. He promised her that one day he was going to be a richer, younger version of Donald Trump. Except for the hair, no one wanted hair like that. Steve's hair implant was guaranteed to look 100% natural for his entire life. In fact, the hair was all Steve's. She shuddered when she thought of them scraping sections of skin off the back of his head and grafting it onto the front. Steve had lots of hair. It went down his neck and onto his shoulders and part way down his back. He'd had electrolysis to remove the hair he didn't want and surgery to move the hair he wanted.

Four years of surgery changed him completely. He didn't resemble the man she married, but he was the man she was married to.

The air in the tube changed. It was thicker, even warmer now. Tiny prickles of warmth penetrated her inside and out simultaneously. She closed her eyes and relaxed into the light. A thick, luscious feeling started at her scalp and worked its way down her body. The light penetrated every nerve, every cell of her body. The scar on her face tingled and the feeling was gone. She realized the scar on her abdomen, a slight reminder of an appendectomy years previous, had done the same. For a moment she felt the same sensation on a small spot on her toe where she'd once had a wart removed. Then, the door in front of her opened.

Now she was the one being escorted away. She looked over to see where Steve was. He exited his tube and was being led away to the green door. Hazel watched him go as she was led to the red door. She waved to him as the doors closed.

This room was much larger than the first. There were comfortable chairs, people milling about, laughing and joking. There was a family in the corner hugging each other, a baby held snugly on a mother's hip.

Hazel searched for Steve. Maybe the green door was for men. She realized this was a false assumption as half the people in the room she was in were men. It wasn't age or hair colour or race or height or weight either. Hazel found one of the slender creatures and approached it.

She pointed to her wedding ring, "Do you know where my husband is?" The creature smiled and nodded and pointed towards a large window at the end of the room. Hazel tried not to run as she made her way through the milling crowd. There, on the other side of the glass, was another room with no visible means of entrance. She cupped her hands around her eyes and peered into the crowd. Finally, she spotted Steve and banged against the window.

"Steve! I'm over here, honey. Steve! Can you hear me?!" A hand gently grabbed her wrist and pulled it away from the pane. Steve never looked over. He never saw her. She felt panic rise in her throat and looked into the creature's eyes.

"Why isn't my husband here with me? Why can't he hear me? What are you doing with us?" Hazel's voice grew louder and shriller and she realized she on the verge of panic.

A white-haired man appeared out of nowhere and took her by the elbow. "We have to talk. Follow me, we'll find a quieter place." Hazel noticed another door at the opposite end of the room. People were hugging and stepping through as families. They were on their way home.

"Where is my husband? Where is Steve?" The man patted a cushioned seat.

"Sit down dear, I'll explain everything." He sat down and waited for her.

"But I don't understand? There are other families here, other people with their loved ones, why can't I be with Steve? Where are you taking us?" Hazel began to twist the bottom of her shirt.

"Hazel; can I call you Hazel? My name is Roger, and I'm an interpreter for our hosts." Roger leaned forward, took Hazel's hand away from her shirt and held it between his. "A long time ago, when our ancestors came here, they looked much like these svelte beings you see before you now. They interbred, lived and worked amongst the Neanderthal people who lived on this earth and eventually became homo sapiens; what we now know as humans. For hundreds of thousands of centuries, our ancestors' progeny have monitored us. They watched how this new race grew, how it evolved, how we became who we are. They watched with sadness as we polluted our oceans, rivers and lakes. It shocked them to see how quickly we fouled our air, destroyed our forests. They watched helplessly as we expanded our technology faster than we expanded our consciousness. They are here to save us from ourselves Hazel, but even their technology can't fix everything we've done."

Hazel stared at the man. "Sir, I mean Roger, what does all this have to do with my husband? Where is Steve? What is the difference between the red door and the green door?" Hazel pulled her hand away and wiped a tear away from her cheek. "Just tell me what is going on."

Roger took a deep breath and continued. "Our cousins, if you don't mind me calling them that, these creatures, they have great technology. They took everything into account when they planned our return home. They knew they could only take home those of us who were direct descendants of their ancestors. There are few of the evolved Neanderthal earth species left, ones that didn't interbreed with aliens. They evolved differently than us. They are blinded by their goals and cannot foresee consequences to their actions. They cannot be allowed to come to our home. The tube and light machine you passed through scanned you to see if you had the correct genes."

Hazel looked stunned. "You mean to tell me my husband isn't coming because he's a purebred? You can't do that! You can't just keep him here and separate us like that!"

Roger cleared his throat. "No, not at all. Your husband was a fine specimen of interbreeding. He had in him the best of both species. It was the alterations, the difference between his DNA, his genes, and his physical appearance. The machines couldn't reconcile what he should look like, compared to what he is now."

Hazel looked around the room. She looked over to one of the creatures by the entrance door. She studied it and noted there was no hair on its head. It had a slender chest, a slightly round belly, and sleepy looking eyes. "Are you saying he could come if he hadn't changed? Can't they just reverse it, can't they see it's him! I have pictures, look, let me show you pictures of before." Hazel pulled her wallet out of her bag and showed a photo to Roger.

"See, it's him. I can vouch for him; I can tell them. Let me tell them it's Steve. Please Roger, please?" Roger handed back the wallet and did not look at the photograph.

"Hazel, it isn't that simple. The transport machines only work within certain parameters. When our cousins built these machines, they took many things into consideration. They understand things happen to our bodies. They knew about appendicitis and tonsillitis and ruptured spleens and c-sections and hysterectomies and dozens of other operations we may encounter in our lives to help us live. They factored it all in and found that in 99.99% of all cases there is a maximum of 10% change in total body structure from what we were born with. A change from what our genes say we should look like. This is their safety net, to make sure that only their ancestors came home with them. They developed this machine to scan us, to look for outsiders."

Roger paused. "They can take us home Hazel; home where we'll have a chance to live. We don't have to stay here and die." Roger stood and paced in front of her.

"When you went through the cleansing tube, it did more than rid your body of viruses and parasites. It scanned you and made a comparison between your genes and your physical appearance. The machine healed you. Any minor scar, or common operation, these things were healed in you, in that tube. Once you stepped through that door, you were as whole a person as if nothing had happened to you since the day you were born. You now have the body you were born to be in; all its bits and pieces. Isn't it wonderful? We'll age much slower and we'll never get sick, Hazel. This is it. This is what we have to live in for a very, very long time."

Hazel cleared her throat and looked around the room. "Are you telling me that my scar is gone?" She ran a finger across her cheek and found unblemished skin. She pulled off her shoe and sock and stared at the bottom of her foot. She hiked up her shirt and pushed down the band of her pants.

"There are no scars. There's nothing there, like it never happened." Hazel put her shoe back on, stood up and grabbed Roger by his shoulders.

"What has happened to Steve?" Hazel let go of the man's shoulders and slumped back in her chair. "I want to see my husband."

Roger sat beside her and straightened his shirt. "Hazel, you won't be seeing Steve again. He's staying here, on Earth. There are limits to what they can do. Anything more than a 10% change in body structure is impossible to reverse." Your husband must have had more than a few minor surgeries."

Hazel nodded, thinking of the hundreds of thousands

of dollars spent on making her husband the perfect man.

Roger continued. "There is too much of a risk if they transport him without reversing what's been done. They can't reverse what's been done without causing him serious damage. Even if we took him as is, the transport machines wouldn't be able to put him back together the same way he is now. The green door was for those who have to go back to Earth, Hazel. Steve won't be coming with us."

Hazel tasted bile in her throat. She couldn't be sick, not here, not now. "Are you telling me that because my husband had surgery, he can't come with us?"

Roger nodded. "It wasn't just the surgery. It was the kind of surgery. All those surgeries, they changed his body more that 10%. Surgery was meant to repair broken bones or a faulty heart valve or save a life. It should never have been used to change what DNA has patterned for us. It should never change the genetic look of what our parents gave us. Those things can't be reversed; the technology just can't handle it." Roger watched Hazel closely.

Hazel's voice was much softer now. "How much longer do you think the planet can support them, the ones that go back? Who will look after the machines that have kept the ice away? When it all breaks down, how much longer before the ice covers the entire planet?"

"I don't have those answers," Roger said as he stood up. He reached for Hazel's hand. "It's time, Hazel. They aren't any more people coming. Not from here. There's nothing more to be done."

Hazel stood as one of the cousins appeared and put a loving arm around her. She followed numbly as the people filed through the final door home. She glanced over at the window and caught a glimpse of Steve. He was talking to the buxom blonde that had gone through before her. He was gesturing at her breasts, pointing to his chin and his pecs, and laughing.

Hazel took one final look at her perfect man and stepped into her future.

The Crutch

Jeremy grunted as he bent to grab the last bag of garbage. Getting old sucked, that plus the only job he could get was as a night cleaner at Tim Hortons—Canada's answer to God as a fast food coffee shop.

He pushed open the back door and wrestled the large bag outside. The streetlight next to the alley made a low buzzing sound, flickered, and went out, plunging him into darkness.

"Damn," he muttered.

His heart beat faster, his hands shook, and sweat dripped into his eyes. He dropped the bag of garbage and leaned against the wall to stop the alley from spinning.

"Not again," he whimpered and grabbed his chest. He closed his eyes and focused on his breathing. Damn panic attacks. They struck at the oddest times.

Jeremy felt his way along the dumpster and found the latch. He lifted the lid and managed to maneuverer the bag up and over the side of the dumpster. He let the lid slam down with a satisfying thud. In the darkness he made his way towards the back door and felt something hit his shins. He lurched forward and found himself spread eagle on the filthy asphalt.

"Arg!" Jeremy rolled over, pushed himself up into a sitting position against the wall, and then inched his way into a standing position.

"What the hell?" He reached down and picked up a wooden crutch. The padding on top was pock marked and smelled like rotting fish. The rubber piece that would normally be on the bottom was gone and only the blunted nub remained.

Jeremy found the back door of Tim Hortons, went inside and examined the crutch. It reminded him of his old friend Simon's crutches. He turned the crutch upside down and looked closely at the worn wood. There, carved into the underside of the hand rest, were the initials S.O.T.

Simon Olaf Thomson. He hadn't thought of him in forty years, or was it forty-five? Simon and Jeremy had once been friends. Simon had something wrong with his leg and needed crutches to get around. Jeremy's mother said they made a great pair because Jeremy had something wrong with his head. Jeremy had a panic attack at least twice a day as an adolescent. As an adult, he'd gone to therapy to learn how to handle them, but even with all his tools he couldn't hold down a job. His mother tried to help by getting Jeremy pets, but they all disappeared. First it was a goldfish, then two hamsters, a guinea pig, and a one-eyed stray cat. All gone.

But Simon stuck around. Good old limp-legged Simon

was oddly comforting during his panic attacks. He watched quietly as Jeremy grabbed his chest and tried to regulate his breath. When it was over, Jeremy was limp and sweaty.

One night before they started their last year of high school, Simon suggested they go for a night hike above the dump. Jeremy agreed as Simon needed him to help manoeuvre the inclines and Simon was there for Jeremy in case of a panic attack. They reached the top of the hill and made their way into the restricted area where the dump trucks emptied out their loads onto the heaps of rotting refuse below.

"This is it," Simon proclaimed. The lights of their small town twinkled in the distance. "This is where I strangled them." Simon spoke in an eerily calm tone.

"Where you what?" Jeremy took a step back and looked at his friend.

Simon lifted one of his crutches to point down below. "I strangled them, and then I tossed them over the edge. No one ever goes down into that mess."

Jeremy's pulse quickened. "Strangled who?"

"Your hamsters, your guinea pig, your cat, and a few other strays I found."

Jeremy started to shake. "Oh, dear God, not now!" he said as Simon closed the gap between them.

"You shouldn't have to live like this Jeremy. I can help." Jeremy froze. Simon leaned his crutches against the railing

Read My Shorts

and placed both hands around Jeremy's neck. He was surprisingly strong. "It only hurts for a little bit." Jeremy flailed at Simon and then pushed as hard as he could. He heard an astonished "No!" and a few seconds later a muffled thump. Jeremy sank to the ground and imagined himself staring at the twinkling lights of his town. When he opened his eyes, all that he saw was one of Simon's crutches. Jeremy tossed it over the edge and ran all the way home.

Some forty years later, at a Tim Hortons, Jeremy was again looking at one of Simon's crutches. He shuddered, went to his happy place, and then decided to throw it away and forget all over again. He opened the back door and headed towards the dumpster. There was a whistling sound of something slicing through the air just before everything went black.

* * *

The smell of decaying donuts and coffee grounds assaulted him as he regained consciousness. A sliver of daylight shone between the dumpster and the lid. He heard the garbage truck, then felt the dumpster shudder as it was lifted high in the air.

He tried to get up but couldn't. Each leg was jammed between the top and the handhold of a crutch. He banged on the dumpster to no avail. Over in the corner he heard someone laugh and saw Simon. Forty-five years dead Simon. What the hell was going on?

Jeremy felt the dumpster shift as the garbage, along with him and the crutches, plummeted into the bowels of the truck. He felt Simon's hand on his shoulder.

"Don't worry, Jeremy, it only hurts for a bit."

Jeremy screamed as the compactor was put into gear and compressed everything around him. He heard his bones snap. Simon was right, it only hurt for a bit.

The Utah Den

Rosemary Wells paced the hallway outside the hotel manager's office at the Utah Den. The period-themed hotel had each of its twelve floors dedicated to the style of that decade, ranging from 1870 to 1980. Her room was on the 1920s floor, in the 1920 themed room. She practically lived here, and she made sure that everything in the room was exactly as she wanted. Only today, it wasn't.

The door to the office opened. A server exited carrying a stack of new menus. Rosemary slipped in before the door closed and stood in front of Mr. Jason Whitaker's desk. She was furious.

"Someone moved my antique dresser to the other side of the room, again!" She loved seeing that old dresser. It calmed her and reminded her of days gone by, a time when life was simpler.

"Did you hear me?" Rosemary bent and leaned on the desk. She glared at Mr. Whitaker as she spoke. "I said, someone has moved my dresser again. This has to stop."

Mr. Whitaker looked up from his computer, pulled his glasses down to the tip of his nose, and squinted at her. He sighed, pushed his glasses up to their proper position, and picked up the phone.

"Hello Margery, it's Mr. Whitaker. Someone moved the dresser in room 1920. It must have been one of the new hires. You know what happens when that darn dresser isn't in the right spot." There was a pause as Margery said something. "Yes, make sure it is positioned just to the left of the bay window. Please get someone to help you move it." Mr. Whitaker hung up the phone and looked in Rosemary's direction. He pulled his glasses back down to the tip of his nose, peered over them and gently squeezed his eyes almost closed.

"Please accept our apologies, Miss Wells. We have new staff for the busy season, they must have moved it. I promise you; it won't happen again."

Rosemary took her hands off his desk, stood and straightened out her dress, then nodded at him. "Thank you, Mr. Whitaker. I appreciate your assistance with this, and I accept your apology." With that, she turned and left the office. Her mood lifted and she decided today would be a perfect day to wander through the new historic art exhibit in the ballroom on the main floor.

Rosemary loved living at the Utah Den. While not the finest hotel in the city, it was the oldest. Some of the rooms reminded her of her childhood and a time when life made more sense. The wide furniture in the 1892 made her feel claustrophobic. She liked the art nouveau look of the 1904 room, and the French panels in the 1911 room were very ornate. However, at the end of the day, it was 1920 she loved the most. Possibly because it was her old dresser that was in that room. A special piece of her family's past to remind her of her roots.

As she entered the ballroom a sense of wonder washed over her. Oil paintings dating back to the late 1800s graced the interior of the room. She stopped in front of the first one. It was quite a busy piece. A happy father, sitting on a table cutting a slice of bread; a mother in a rocking chair holding a baby; and a child about to eat a piece of bread. In the lower left corner was a cat on a trunk. It was tied to some sort of metal container with a golden string. She examined the piece more closely. How odd that someone would tie up a cat like that. Then she noticed a wood stove in pieces on the floor and dishes in a basket under the table. The room looked rather shabby, but the people looked happy enough. There was a pitcher and a glass of beer on the table to the right of the mother. "Maybe they're drunk," she muttered to herself.

"Oh, I hardly think so." A deep voice rumbled near her left ear.

"Excuse me?" Rosemary took a step back to get a closer look at the man who had quietly insinuated himself into her space.

"It's called, *Just Moved*, by Henry Mosler." The baritone voice slipped out through the man's barely parted lips and into Rosemary's ear. A slight shiver of pleasure ran down her spine. He was dressed rather nicely in a tailcoat and carrying a fashionable cane. His skin was the colour of coffee with fresh cream, just the way she liked it. He wore an old-fashioned top hat, too. Perhaps he was dressed this way in honour of the exhibit.

"Oh, I see," Rosemary said, now understanding why the room in the painting was in such disarray. A warmth came over her as she stepped away from the stranger.

"I'm so sorry. I didn't mean to upset you." The man smiled and Rosemary immediately felt at ease. "Allow me to introduce myself. I am Baron La Croix. I'm visiting from down south and heard about the exhibit. It's fascinating isn't it?"

Rosemary let herself relax. "Yes, yes, it is." She stared at the painting again. "I think I recognize that cupboard. Or is it an armoire? It looks like the one in room 1871."

"You have a fine eye for antiques." He let his hand brush up against hers as he made his way to the next painting. Rosemary blushed and felt herself moving in his wake. The pair walked silently from painting to painting, looking at each other now and then.

"Rosemary?" the hotel manager called. "Rosemary? Are you in here?"

Rosemary stepped back from the painting and stood directly in front of the manager. She swore the man was blind as a bat, always peering at her over the top of his glasses.

"I'm right here, Mr. Whitaker. What on earth is the matter?"

He stared straight at her, then lowered his glasses and squinted. "Ah, there you are." He looked past Rosemary, squinted again and smiled. "Ah, Monsieur La Croix. We are so thankful you could make it. Your room will be ready in just a few minutes. It's 1952." He handed La Croix his key card.

La Croix nodded and smiled. "This lovely lady has been keeping me company."

"This lady has a name," Rosemary huffed.

"Apologies again dear lady, but may I point out you have yet to introduce yourself." La Croix smiled and Rosemary felt another shudder, accompanied by a slight twinge in her nether regions. What on earth was happening to her?

"Oh my," she stammered. "Now it's my turn to apologize. There seems to be a lot of that going around today. I am so sorry. I'm Rosemary, Rosemary Wells. I live in the 1920 room."

La Croix smiled, gave a slight bow, then took Rosemary's hand and kissed it. "Enchanté Mademoiselle."

Rosemary felt the strength go out of her calf muscles and her knees threatened to buckle. She quickly retrieved her hand and looked at the hotel manager.

"Well?" She waited for him to announce his reason for seeking her out.

"It's about your room," he said. "With it being the busy season, and this new art exhibit, we are completely booked up. We had to rent your room to a nice couple from Victoria, BC. They'll be checking in within the hour."

"What!" Rosemary was shocked. "You can't do that. That's my room!"

"Well, Ms. Wells, you haven't actually paid for the room, so we do have the right to rent it out." Mr. Whitaker sighed, then narrowed his eyes again, trying to see Rosemary in the subdued lighting.

"What? No, that can't be right!" Rosemary tried to think back when she had made a payment. Wasn't it just the other week, or was it last month? "Well, you wouldn't let me stay here for free. I'm sure I've paid. This is ridiculous!"

La Croix stepped in front of the hotel manager. "Allow me to take it from here," he said.

Mr. Whitaker sighed again. "Well, let's hope you can get through to her." He pushed his glasses up with his index finger and turned to leave.

"Wait!" Rosemary cried. "My things! My dresser! You can't let strangers paw through my delicates!"

"Bring her dresser and her things to my room." La Croix said this with such authority that Rosemary did not argue.

Mr. Whitaker pulled down his glasses to the tip of his nose and tried to focus in on La Croix. "Pardon me?"

"Her things. Everything. Have it moved to my room.

Now. The lady can have my bed and I assume there is a cot or hide-a-bed for me."

"Why yes, of course," Mr. Whitaker said. He nodded, turned and disappeared out the door.

Rosemary inhaled sharply and pulled herself up to her full height. "I hardly know you, sir. I deeply doubt we should be sharing a room," she said indignantly, however; deep down she was thrilled to have been rescued by this dark and mysterious gentleman. She was still perplexed as to how she could have forgotten to pay for the room, but one look into La Croix's eyes made her forget her current predicament.

"Let's look at more of these paintings, shall we?" La Croix took her arm and led her to a painting from 1920.

Rosemary gasped when she saw it. "Oh, my goodness. That's my dresser!"

La Croix smiled and slipped his arm around her shoulder. "And is that you kneeling in front of it, putting away your finery?"

Rosemary looked closer at the painting. The woman's back was to the viewer and she appeared to be on her knees sorting through things in the bottom drawer. A beautiful antique clock sat atop the dresser. To the left was a carved wooden chair with an upholstered cushion. Behind the chair, a gentle light streamed through what appeared to be a large glass door. She looked at the sign below the painting:

Robert Panitzsch, Interior with Young Woman.

"Of course, it's not me, but that's my dresser. You'll see when they bring it to your room," she said, sealing her fate for the evening.

"Ah, then you accept my offer." La Croix took his arm away from her shoulder and turned her to face him. "I think the room should be ready now, let's see if they have all your things there."

Rosemary looked deep into his eyes and took his hand. A stream of excitement flowed through her. She'd never been alone in a room with a man before, or had she? What would her father think? Where was her father?

The pair breezed past the front desk and took the elevator to the ninth floor. La Croix pulled out his key card and opened the door. A bright green striped hide-a-bed sat along the far wall. Across from that was a cobalt blue coffee table and two short-back upholstered chairs in the same blue. Near the door, two bright red upholstered metal chairs sat on either side of a small Formica and chrome table. The bed had a short white headboard and a shorter footboard with a quilted green bedspread on top. Beside her dresser stood a squat wooden chest of drawers. Her ornate dresser looked out of place here. Her hairbrush and silver hand mirror were atop her dresser along with her manicure kit and her face cream in her sterling dresser jar.

As Rosemary explored the room, La Croix placed his

hat, coat and cane in the closet. He took off his tie and unbuttoned the top three buttons of his shirt, then stood beside the bed.

When Rosemary looked at him, her breath caught in her throat. La Croix was a fine specimen of a man. Light from the window gleamed off his muscled chest. Rosemary remembered to breathe and stepped as far away from the bed as possible.

"Don't be frightened," he said. In the blink of an eye he was beside her. He wrapped one arm around her waist and cupped her chin with his free hand. "I'm going to kiss you now," he said.

Rosemary closed her eyes and felt his warm lips press against hers. Her loins caught fire and within seconds she was kissing him back with a hunger she'd never known before.

La Croix released her and laughed. It wasn't a cruel laugh. It was a deep belly laugh of someone who was genuinely happy and amused all at once.

Rosemary smiled as he led her towards the bed. "I've never, I mean this is my," her voice trailed off and La Croix kissed her again. She pulled away. "I'm a virgin!"

"I know my dear," he said as he started to undress her. "I believe that's why you're stuck here." He kissed her neck as he slipped her dress off her shoulders and let it fall to the floor. He deftly removed her bra with his left hand, then his right hand slid her panties off. He picked her up and laid her gently on the gaudy green bedspread. She tried to cover herself, but he stopped her. Before she knew it, he was naked and lying beside her.

La Croix's kisses ignited her passion and she found her body arching towards him.

"Oh my," she managed to blurt out between kisses. La Croix's hands were doing things to her that she only did to herself, in the dark, under the covers.

La Croix eased up on his kisses and looked deeply into her eyes as he shifted his body atop hers. "Just relax sweet Rosemary. Soon you'll be free."

Rosemary gasped as they joined together. All her senses exploded in a brilliant flash of light. She had never felt so alive.

A few hours later there was a knock at the door. Mr. James Whitaker and Margery from housekeeping entered the room. Mr. Whitaker looked around, his glasses down around the tip of his nose, his eyes narrowed as if trying to focus on something.

"Do you see her?" Margery asked. "Or him? Do you see him?"

Mr. Whitaker shook his head, "No."

"Oh, thank the Lord!" Margery proclaimed as she gathered up Rosemary's belongings from atop the dresser and in the drawers. "I'll have someone move the dresser back to 1920 right away," she said as she closed the bag of Rosemary's belongings. "How did you know?" she asked as Mr. Whitaker opened the door.

"I did some research," he said. "I discovered that a Miss Rosemary Wells died in what is now room 1920. Her family had rented out four rooms on the fifth floor for the summer. She'd snuck in a gentleman caller and was about to have sexual relations with him, when her father burst in with a gun. Rosemary tried to stop him and was killed instantly."

"And La Croix?" she asked. "How on earth were you able to summon a Haitian Creole spirit to seduce her."

"She's gone, that's all you need to know." Mr. Whitaker pushed his glasses back up onto the bridge of his nose and closed the door.

The Will

Felicity Rathbone bustled past the doorman and into the foyer of the von Heka mansion. She was on a mission. Hildegard von Heka was her neighbor and the best psychic in the county. She was the only one who could answer Felicity's question. She swore if she didn't get an answer soon the stress would kill her. She was hoping she could contact Frank's ghost and put the matter to rest for once and for all.

She paid no attention to who was there as she maneuvered her way through the dozen or so dinner party guests making their way towards the formal dining room. They took their time, milling about, chatting and laughing, while Felicity went straight to the head of the table where a rather stoic looking young man stared at the crowd.

"Excuse me." Felicity placed herself squarely in front of the lad. "I need to speak to Hildegard, and I need to speak to her now."

The young man slowly looked at her and cocked his head to the side. "Ah, Mrs. Rathbone. We weren't expecting you; however, we are always glad to entertain unexpected guests. We keep this seat open, just in case. My name is Trevor, I am Madam von Heka's personal assistant. She'll be here momentarily. Please, sit." He pointed to a chair to the left of the head of the table.

Felicity made some harrumphing noises as she waited for the chair to be pulled out for her. Trevor ignored her, so she pulled out the chair and sat. She would speak to Hildegard about her assistant's lack of manners. She wondered why she hadn't seen him before.

She'd met Hildegard a little over two years ago at a dinner party, much like this one. Only that time the party was at Felicity's home and they were trying to summon the spirit of Frank, her recently departed husband. And while Frank did make a brief appearance, Hildegard told her the newly dead were rather hesitant to talk to the living.

For now, Felicity was living in the home they had shared, and she had a generous monthly stipend, along with some art and investments. Frank's three adult children from his first marriage, were given smaller properties, a winter house, a cottage and a farm, as well as a few thousand dollars in stocks and bonds. Frank's children had contested the will since the day after he died. They were convinced their father had a different will: one where they got everything.

Felicity was the first to admit that life with Frank had not been great during his last year. She had no idea how to cope with his failing health. At first, she would go away for a day or two, and near the end, for weeks at a time. She left Frank in the care of his nurses and his children.

Felicity learned of his death while on a retreat in the Adaman Islands off the coast of Thailand. By the time she arrived home, Frank's children had already contested the will. Felicity had spent the last two years in and out of court whilst fiercely hanging on to what she believed to be rightfully hers. After all, she'd spent a good ten years of her life with Frank. They'd still be together if he hadn't hated doctors. By the time they found the cancer, it was too late.

Now, here she was, barging in on a dinner party to ask a psychic if there was a newer will. Yesterday morning had been the last straw. Frank's children dropped a new lawsuit on her, suing her for all their legal expenses. The stress of it was aggravating her heart palpitations. She was more than ready to rid herself of Frank's kids and live out the rest of her life in peace.

A couple in their late thirties approached the head of the table. The woman sat beside Felicity and the man across from her. Felicity ignored them and motioned Trevor over.

"How much longer will she be?" Felicity touched her chest and was happy to note the palpitations had abated.

"Just a moment more, ma'am. I assure you. She'll be pleasantly surprised to learn you are here." Trevor stepped back and stared into space.

Felicity had no choice but to wait. She'd spent the last 734 days fighting to keep what Frank left to her. Frank's children never liked her. It started when Frank convinced her to elope to Jamaica after three months of dating. Now his kids wanted to take away the mansion, the trust fund, the artwork, everything.

"Screw them," she muttered under her breath. Trevor stopped his space-staring vigil and gave her a slight scowl.

All the guests were seated now. Most of them looked expectantly towards the side entrance of the dining room. A moment later, Madam Hildegard von Heka appeared, dressed in a simple cream-colored floor-length dress. Her hair was swept up in a bun with loose curls falling about her aging face. She looked each guest in the eye, smiled, and nodded. Felicity noted that Trevor didn't pull the chair out for her either.

"Thank you all for coming tonight," she said as she took her seat. Trevor bent over and whispered in her ear. The psychic smiled. "It appears we have an unexpected guest this evening, Mrs. Felicity Rathbone."

The guests oohed and aahed, their eyes turning towards Felicity. She smiled, somewhat taken aback by the attention.

"Why thank you, Hildegard. I wasn't expecting such a warm welcome." Felicity nodded to her host.

"We'll let Mrs. Rathbone get settled in before we get to the questions. Now, let's eat and enjoy the feast my staff has prepared for you."

Sharply dressed servants appeared bearing trays weighed down with assorted meats and sauces, vegetable dishes, soups and salads. Muted conversations bubbled up from the far end of the table. Snippets of laughter mixed with the sound of cutlery gently clinked against bone china. No one paid the slightest bit of attention to Felicity.

Hildegard motioned to a server to create an extra plate for Felicity. They placed an assortment of dishes in front of her. Felicity took a sniff and smiled.

"This smells delicious," she said.

She really wasn't that hungry, so she pushed the food around her plate and tried to blend in with the guests. She turned to the woman beside her.

"So, how do you know Hildegard?" she asked.

The woman ignored her, leaned forward to hear something her male companion said, then laughed. Felicity couldn't quite make out what they were saying. Damn tinnitus. She'd have to call her doctor in the morning and get her hearing checked. It had gotten worse since the latest court document was delivered.

She motioned for Trevor to come closer. "Can I ask my question now?" she asked.

"Tell me," he said. "I'll pass it along."

"Why can't I just ask her myself?" Felicity protested. "I'm three feet away."

Trevor ignored her, walked over to Hildegard and whispered in her ear.

"It appears our guest of honour also has a question," Hildegard said as she pushed away her almost empty plate.

"I don't care what she wants," said a voice from the

far end of the table. "It's been two long years. We need to know, especially now. Did my father have a newer will?" It was Marjorie, Frank's oldest.

Felicity leaned forward. "That's my question, too," Felicity said as she stared down the long table. She recognized Evan and Sam, Frank's boys, sitting with Marjorie.

"I think it's time to contact Frank and put this matter to rest." Hildegard motioned for the staff to clear the plates.

"Yes," Felicity said. "I whole heartedly agree."

Trevor smiled and bent over to whisper in Hildegard's ear.

"Well Marjorie, it appears our guest agrees and is anxious to know the answer as well," Hildegard said.

"Why on earth would she care about that?" Marjorie asked. "It's a bit redundant, don't you think?" A nervous twitter went through the crowd, not sure if they should laugh at the boorish joke.

Felicity glared at Marjorie. That shrew was getting on her last nerve. Marjorie knew damn well why Felicity cared. Two years of hell and court battles, that's why. Her poor heart couldn't take much more.

"Well, let's find out." Hildegard leaned back and let her head rest against the high-backed chair. "Frank, are you with us?"

Trevor moved to stand behind Felicity. She dared not turn around. The thought of seeing her dead husband sent a chill through her. She really should have been there for him. He had told her to take some time away, at least the first time. The rest of the mini escapes had been her idea. She was gone for six of the twelve months before he died. It just felt so good to get out and away from all that sickness. She made a face as she recalled the scent in his room: part fresh linen, part soup, and part decay. Cancer really was a bitch.

Trevor walked back to Hildegard and whispered in her ear. Hildegard nodded and glanced past Felicity.

"Frank's here," the psychic announced. Felicity sat up straighter, afraid to turn around. "And he has answers. There was another will. However, the only difference was an added clause that stipulated all monies, all property, and all investments would revert back to his children upon Felicity's death."

A murmur went through the crowd. Marjorie stood, placed her hands firmly on the table, and stared at Hildegard. "Well then, where the hell is it? We need it now more than ever."

Felicity frowned at Marjorie. She never understood how such a rude cow could be Frank's eldest. If Felicity had her way, his kids would get nothing. They'd made her life a living hell. But if the new will meant she could live out her life in peace, so be it. Felicity had no children of her own and would have left it all to charity. A smile formed on her lips. The relief that her battle had ended slowly washed over her. Maybe now she could relax and not have to deal with her shitty step-kids.

Hildegard held up her hand, motioning that she had more to say. "The newer will is in the library, in a false drawer in Frank's desk. The top drawer, right hand side."

The group clapped softly and whispered to each other. Sam stood. "Finally. I'll head over there now and call you as soon as I find it. I'll break the damn desk open with an ax if I have to."

"You'll do no such thing," Felicity shouted. "That's my house."

"Now, Sam, there will be no need for that," Hildegard chided. "Be quick about it, though. It's there, just pull out the drawer, flip it over, and open it. We'll wait here for your call."

"Like hell he will. It's still my house. I'll go get it." Felicity pushed back her chair, stood, turned and gasped. Frank stood in her way. It was Frank, only it wasn't Frank. He was younger, like when they'd first met. He was healthy, too. Confused, she turned to Trevor. "How? I mean, can everyone else see him, too?"

"No, ma'am," Trevor said. "Just me and you."

"Hello Felicity." Frank took a step towards her. "I didn't think I'd see you again this soon."

"Can Hildegard see him?" Felicity asked, not

understanding why she could see and hear Frank. Maybe it was a spouse thing.

"No ma'am. That's what I'm here for. I relay messages from the other side. Hildegard was my mother. We have a strong connection."

"Was?" Felicity took a step towards Frank.

"Yes," Trevor said. "I crossed over unexpectedly fifteen years ago. We've been working together ever since."

Felicity stared at Trevor, then looked at Frank. "I'm not sure I understand. I thought Hildegard could ... I mean ... "

Frank reached for Felicity and held her hand. "It's okay, dear. It was lonely without you. But now, this ..." his voice trailed off. "Well, I'm glad you're here now."

Felicity stood rooted to the floor. This was all too much. A cell phone rang at the far end of the room. Marjorie answered it.

"Hello?" Every guest at the table held their breath. "He found it," she announced. "Just where Dad said it would be. The estate, everything reverts to the three of us now." Marjorie's eyes misted up. "Thank you, so, so much, Hildegard."

"What does she mean by now?" Felicity turned away from Frank, his hand still holding hers. "Hildegard, what did she mean? Why won't you talk to me? Anybody? Can you hear me?" Felicity didn't feel well, not well at all. The buzzing in her ears intensified. "Trevor, you can hear me.

What's going on here?"

Trevor rushed to Hildegard's side and whispered in her ear.

"Ladies and gentlemen." Hildegard stood. "It appears our guest doesn't know she's passed over."

Felicity gasped. "Who doesn't know? Me? Don't be foolish. Trevor, tell her. I'm right here."

Felicity thought about the last few days. She'd been dizzy and nauseous, and her heart was pounding like crazy. But she was better now. Last night it all stopped, and she felt fine, except for the damn buzzing sound. Frank pulled Felicity closer. "It's okay, it's not that bad, being dead. I think you'll like it. I've so much to show you."

Felicity tried to back away, but Frank held her close. She looked into his eyes and felt a calmness flow over her. Her body felt weightless. Then, the buzzing in her ears stopped.

"How about that?" she said. "The buzzing stopped." She smiled at her husband. "Is it true, am I really dead?"

Frank nodded and held her close as a bright light appeared in front of them. Felicity smiled and she and Frank stepped towards it.

Trevor whispered into his mother's ear.

"Well, that's that then," Hildegard said. "Never a dull moment. Let's retire to the sitting room for dessert, shall we?"

Murder in the Cards

Detective Jacoby walked up to the crime scene. The young cop guarding the door was staring at his phone. Jacoby cleared his throat. "Get off the damn phone! What's your name?"

"Simpson, sir. James Simpson." The young officer put his phone away, glanced at Jacoby's ID, and moved aside.

"You can't be a good cop if you don't pay attention, Simpson." Jacoby stepped past Simpson and into the sparsely furnished room. He was getting too old for this. At least they let him work alone now that he was mere months away from retirement. He would have been at the scene sooner, but his damn prostate was acting up and he had to pee before he left the station. Jacoby looked back at Simpson and then at the scene before him.

Another dead guy slumped over another poker table with a set of tongs by his head. There were no cards, money or poker chips on the table. Those had been cleaned up before the 911 call. Gamblers didn't like to implicate themselves when cops were involved. There were several take-away coffee cups on the table, some with lids, some without. Jacoby pulled out his notepad and jotted down the logos on the cups. The place smelled faintly like a cross between a gym locker and coffee shop.

The scene was eerily similar to the last three he'd attended in the past month. On the surface they all looked like heart attacks at a poker game. The toxicology reports said they were poisoned. Probably the same for this poor schmuck. Jacoby knew the other players wouldn't have any idea how the tongs got there. He also suspected that as soon as he looked in the dead guy's mouth, he would find a playing card. The killer definitely had a signature.

"Hey, Simpson!" Jacoby hollered. "Anyone else been in here?"

"Yes, sir. The four other guys playing poker. They're in the room to your left with Officer Campbell. The paramedics are still out by the rig."

"Any of those guys at the last game with a dead guy?"

"No, sir."

"Did the paramedics touch anything?" Jacoby asked as he made some notes.

"Just the body, sir. The guy was cold when they got here."

Jacoby rubbed his hand across his face. He could question the other four poker players, but he knew what they'd say. They met for a game of cards, shortly after they started playing the dead guy felt sick, then collapsed.

Jacoby stepped closer to the corpse. "When is the coroner getting here?" he shouted to Simpson.

"They're a little delayed," Simpson replied. "Should be just a few more minutes."

Jacoby rubbed the back of his neck. Protocol be damned. He didn't want to wait for them.

"Well," he said as he pulled on his latex gloves. "Let's see what you've got." Jacoby gently pried the man's mouth open and pulled out a card. "Ace of diamonds," he said as he unfolded the card. "What the frick does it mean?"

"Excuse me, sir?"

"Just talking to myself, Simpson." Jacoby put the card on the table beside the tongs. "Is forensics on their way, too?"

"Yes, sir," Simpson said. He reached for his phone and tapped away on the small keyboard.

"Damn it!" Jacoby walked over to the young cop. "Put that away!"

"Wait, sir, I have an idea," Simpson said. "I think I have something."

"Really?" Jacoby was getting annoyed.

"The clues, sir," Simpson showed the phone to Jacoby. "See, if you type in ace and tongs into this anagram solver you get new words."

Jacoby stared at the small screen. "So, what's does it say?"

"Well," Simpson said, "there's quite a few: egos cant, cage snot and a con gets."

"Hmmm." Jacoby pondered a moment. "Don't close that down yet. I need to check my notes. The ten, four, queen and now the ace, all diamonds. Type in diamond and tongs. What do you get?"

Jacoby flipped open a clean page in his notebook and waited.

"Well, there's nomads dig not."

Jacoby let out a small growl. This is why he hated working with others. "Damn it, Simpson, tell me something that could be cryptic. This killer wants to show us how smart she is."

"She, sir?" Simpson looked up.

"Poison, Simpson. The number one choice for female serial killers. They found something called taxus baccata in the last three stiffs. It's what makes yew trees toxic. Look for something herbal or medical or like that." Jacoby waited impatiently.

"Okay, well there's Dion Gaston MD?" Simpson smiled. He liked detecting.

Jacoby pulled out his phone and typed in Dion Gaston, MD. There was forty-three Dion Gastons in the city, none of them doctors.

"What else?" Jacoby felt like they were on to something.

"Well, there's dominant gods, but that has nothing to do with herbs or medicine."

"Dominant gods?" Jacoby rubbed his neck again. "Look

up female gods."

"There's Aphrodite and Athena."

"Nah," Jacoby said. "Goddess of love and goddess of wisdom. I don't think the killer identifies with them. What else?"

Simpson looked up from his phone. "There's Hera, the wife of Zeus. Revenge was her thing."

"Revenge." Jacoby paused for a moment. "Get the paramedics and bring them back here."

"Yes, sir." Simpson did as he was told and returned with a man and a woman.

"Just a few questions if you don't mind." Jacoby stood in front of the man. "What's your name?"

"David, David Roy."

"Where were you when the call came in?" Jacoby raised his pen over his notepad.

"We were sitting in the rig drinking coffee. It was break time."

Jacoby looked up. "What type of coffee? Starbucks, Serious, Dunkin, Bean There?"

"Ummm, I think it was Bean There. First time, too. Coffee is pretty good. My partner recommended it."

Jacoby glanced at the other paramedic. "Once you got here, did you ever leave your partner alone with the body?"

"No, sir, we left together. Well, I left first and then she came out a few seconds later."

Jacoby nodded and stepped in front of the woman. "And you, what's your name?"

"Rhea," she replied, as she tried to look past the detective.

Detective Jacoby's eyes lit up. "Nice name."

At that moment, the forensics team arrived, glanced at Jacoby and headed for the murder scene.

"Not so fast," Jacoby said. "I need you to bag and tag every single coffee cup in there, and any you find outside and in the paramedics' rig. I need the contents tested and fingerprints from all of them." The lead on the team nodded and motioned to another team member to do it. Jacoby turned his attention back to Rhea.

"So, tell me, Rhea, why'd you go to the coffee shop?"

"No reason. It was new and I'd heard the coffee was great." She looked at Jacoby and then over to Simpson.

"Yeah, a good cuppa coffee is important in our jobs."

Jacoby gave her his best fake smile. Rhea appeared to relax a bit.

"Just a few more questions, Rhea." Jacoby glanced down at his notebook. "Did you touch anything other than the dead guy in there."

"No, sir. It was obvious he was dead, so we left as soon as we couldn't find a pulse. Guy was cold. There was no need to try and revive him." Rhea shifted from one foot to another. "Is that all?"

"Nope, just a few more things I need to clear up." Jacoby closed his notebook and took a step towards Rhea. "My notes show you two were on scene for the other three suspected heart attacks. Were you the last to leave the room at all the other locations?"

"Ummm, I don't know, maybe." Rhea glanced towards her partner. "I make sure we pick up all our stuff before we leave."

"Do you live nearby?" Jacoby waited for an answer and then interrupted her before she could speak. "Forget about that, tell me, do you have a home with trees on the property?"

Rhea looked over to Simpson and back to Jacoby. "We used to. The bank foreclosed on our house six months ago. What does this have to do with anything?"

"Is your husband a gambler?" Jacoby leaned forward slightly. The blood drained from Rhea's face. "Just two more questions. Were they yew trees? And how did you track down the men who cheated your husband out of your life savings?"

Rhea bolted for the door. Simpson stopped her before she could leave the building. Jacoby smiled. "Cuff her."

Simpson pulled her arms behind her back and slipped on the cuffs. "How did you know?"

"Yew trees are pretty common around here," Jacoby said. "But most people don't know they are highly toxic.

My guess is that Rhea knew that, and she found out who the guys were that took their life savings. She learned their patterns and plotted her revenge. It would be easy to slip poison into someone's coffee where it wouldn't be detected. Plus, she signed her work with her name."

"Right!" Simpson said. "Hera is an anagram of Rhea!"

"Nice working with you kid," Jacoby smiled as he took Rhea by the elbow and walked her out to the waiting cruiser.

Secret Chef

Ash McKenzie was having a wild dream. In it, she was Supergirl, or Superwoman, or some sort of superhero. The sound of people talking roused her from her sleep. She lifted her head off the counter. Where was she? This wasn't her bedroom. Ash blinked twice and rubbed her eyes. Her classmates and instructor were setting the dishes out for Chef's arrival. Last thing she remembered; she was preparing her selections for judging. Had she fallen asleep last night? The answer was obviously, yes.

These culinary classes were her well-deserved prize. Five neighbouring cities held competitions to find their best home cook. Ash was one of the winners, and now she was here, at these advanced culinary classes to see if she could wow the head chef of Chez Renaurd. This was the last day of classes and whoever won this cook off, would receive a one-year paid apprenticeship. It was a dream come true for Ash, but now the dream was becoming a nightmare. She knew her instructor was counting on her. She'd been an underdog from the start and had proven herself to be worthy of winning. That is, until today. Maybe she could quickly whip something up before Chef arrived.

She ran her hands under the tap at her station sink, splashed her face and ran her wet fingers through her hair. She went to pat her hands on her apron, but it wasn't there.

Her instructor walked up behind her.

"Looking for this?" he said as he lifted the apron from her back. "Are you okay, Ash?"

She nodded, grabbed the apron, and put it on properly as Chef walked through the door.

Ash felt her stomach turn. She had failed. There was no way she could win. She hadn't prepared a single thing, and there was no time to do it now. Chef walked beside the long table at the front of the class. There were ten summer salads and ten desserts all waiting to be sampled. Ash counted them again. That couldn't be right. She hadn't made anything and there were ten people in the class. She stood on tiptoe and counted again. Yep, there were twenty samples ready to be judged. She looked around and then motioned for her instructor to come over.

"I didn't make anything," she said in a whisper.

"What?" the instructor turned around and counted the dishes. "Of course you did, there are twenty dishes up there."

"I fell asleep. It's been an exhausting week, with my son moving out and my cat being sick and my mother moving in. I'm so tired. Whoever made those two dishes up there, it wasn't me." Ash bowed her head in shame.

"Maybe magic fairies came in and made them for you." He winked at Ash and smiled.

"I doubt it," Ash said.

"Maybe the story of the elves and the shoemaker is real!" He laughed and patted Ash on the shoulder, then went up to the table laden with the students' culinary creations. They had done him proud.

Chef had tasted each salad and was almost finished with the desserts. He paused at the last one, smacked his lips and smiled. He strode to the middle of the room and looked at each and every student.

"All of your samples were excellent, but there is one person here who made both the salad and the dessert stand out. The lemon pepper Cali salad sprinkled with fresh calendula and arugula flower petals and the croissant pudding with whiskey caramel sauce. Will my next apprentice please step forward."

No one moved. Ash looked confused. She was going to make the Cali salad and croissant pudding, but she didn't. She couldn't have.

"I believe it's Ash you're looking for, Chef." Her instructor went to her side and pulled her up to the front of the class.

"But ... I didn't ... " Ash stammered. She stood before Chef, a lump in her throat.

"You didn't what?" Chef asked, shaking her hand. "Congratulations Ash. I think this next year is going to be an excellent partnership."

Her instructor held his index finger to his lips, signalling for her to shush.

"I didn't make them!" The words came out much louder than she expected. The class was stunned into silence.

"If you didn't make them, who did?"

A student at the back of the class spoke up. "Check the security footage. This place is wired up like Fort Knox."

Chef nodded. Ash's instructor looked uncomfortable.

"Well, let's do it then," Chef said, and the trio walked across the hall to the instructor's office.

They stood in front of the computer as he pulled up the footage from the night before. There was Ash, head down on the counter, fast asleep. They fast forwarded hour by hour and finally, at five a.m., Ash moved. Not only did she move, she sat up and went straight to the pantry. She returned a few minutes later with an armload of supplies.

They watched as Ash untied the apron from around her waist and flipped it around like a cape. "I'm super chef!" she exclaimed as she pretended to fly around the room, her cape flapping behind her. She stopped in front of her station and proceeded to skilfully create her salad. Once it was complete, she leapt from countertop to countertop, humming the Supergirl theme song.

She jumped down and combined the ingredients for the pudding, adding the whiskey into the caramel sauce. She placed a single mint leaf on top. She took both dishes into the walk-in fridge and returned to her station. She cleaned up, then sat down, put her head on the counter, and fell fast asleep.

Chef turned to her and shook her hand again. "Well," he said, a touch of amusement in his voice. "If you can do that in your sleep, I can't wait to see what you do when you're awake. Welcome aboard."

Survivor

Uki crawled away from camp on her belly, her white parka offering a small level of camouflage. She couldn't spend one more minute on this unstable ice flow. Hell, for all she knew she was on top of the North Pole right now. Spending six months here for a documentary was insanity. The director thought he could have his way with every female in camp and she hadn't slept in days.

She stopped behind a snowbank and double-checked her pack: protein bars, water, things to keep her warm, and tampons. She'd even grabbed the last box of condoms.

Uki was heading to the spot where the Russian's Barneo Ice Camp helicopter brought its cargo of grinning tourists. It was only an hour's walk away. If it didn't come today, it would come tomorrow. To get there all she had to do was head south. She chuckled to herself. Every direction from here was south.

It may have been spring, but it was still damn cold at -11°C. She was sick of the snow, the cold, and the wind. Uki adjusted her purple balaclava and continued her walk. Without warning the snow beneath her gave way. She fell, face first, into a large puddle of cold, mushy salt water.

"Damn it!" she spat out a mouthful of slush and made

her way to a craggy hummock of ice. She pulled off her now frozen boot and damp sock. Then she dried her foot with a fresh sock. She rummaged through her pack and found the box of condoms. She tore into it, pulled one out, and ripped it open. She cautiously fit the condom over her foot and thanked whoever had the foresight and ego to bring extra-large to the camp. She pulled on a dry sock, then another condom, and finally put her boot back on. She did the same to her other foot and then her hands. She'd taken the condoms for spite, but now was glad she had them.

She listened for the helicopter. Nothing—except the endless, relentless wind. She opened three more condoms and stuffed her lighter, matches, tinder, and dry socks into them. She put the last condom in her inside pocket, then smiled and thought, *You never know when you're going to need protection.*

Time to go. Uki walked another forty-five minutes. Small icicles clung to her eyelashes. She found a small snowbank, sat, drank some water, and ate a protein bar. She closed her eyes and listened. Still nothing. If the helicopter didn't come within the hour, she'd have to find a place to sleep for the night.

Uki headed towards a twelve-meter high ice shelf and climbed to the top. There, about fifty meters away, was a spot where snow had been blown into a circular pattern.

This was it. She would wait here. She slid down the ice surface and looked for shelter. There was more open water here than at camp. Damn climate change was turning everything into a melted mess. Uki jumped over a puddle, slipped, and slid straight into the back end of a polar bear.

Bears don't come this far north, she thought. She scrambled backwards as the bear that shouldn't be there turned and roared. She was going to die. The white Arctic killer rose up on its hindquarters. Uki managed to stand and ran towards a crack in the ice shelf. Her knees buckled as the bear ripped open the back of her lower leg with one well-placed swipe. Uki ducked as the bear lunged for her head. It tore the pack from her back as she slipped into the ice crevice. It was a tight fit, but she'd be damned if she was going to be a polar bear's breakfast. She pressed her calf, dripping with blood, against the ice.

The bear charged at the opening. It snapped and chewed at the ice wall; its breath warm on Uki's face. After a few agonizing moments, it stopped. The bear's massive shoulders were too large to fit through the opening. It turned away and tore into Uki's backpack, tossing supplies everywhere. It found the protein bars and sat down to eat.

Uki knew she was done. At least hypothermia was a better way to die than being eaten alive. That is, if she didn't bleed to death first. She pressed her open calf harder into the ice and passed out.

When she came to, the bear was gone. How long had she slept? She took a deep breath and rocked her calf away from the wall. Fresh pain shot through her. She bit her lip and inched her way out of the crevice. No helicopter. She slumped to the ground and crawled to her remaining possessions. There were tampons strewn everywhere. She gathered them up and crawled back to the side of the ice wall.

She took out a tampon and placed it lengthwise into her wound. It expanded and turned the tampon bright red from tip to tail. She needed a tourniquet. Then she remembered the condom. She reached into her pocket and carefully opened the package. She stretched and tied the condom tightly just below her knee. She pulled the bloody tampon out and tossed it aside. Uki winced in pain, took a deep breath and gingerly placed a second and a third tampon into what was once her calf muscle. The tampons began filling with blood, then stopped. It worked. Exhausted and weak, she passed out.

Voices weaved their way through her dreams.

"Whooo hooo! We're at the North Pole!"

She opened one eye and tried to stand.

"Hey, is that a backpack over there?"

"Blood!" another voice said.

"Oh my God, it's a woman!" a third said.

Uki felt herself being carried towards the helicopter.

"Are those tampons?" a voice asked.

"Is that a condom?" someone else asked.

"Yep," she replied weakly.

She'd be home by tomorrow.

Pooper Scooper

"Why do you insist on pooping on the sidewalk?" Gordon asked as he pulled a poop bag from his jacket pocket. The moment he bent over to pick up Bonita's warm and eerily human sized turd, she decided it was time to move on.

"Damn it, Bonita! Stop!" he screamed and yanked the leash. The eight-month old bull mastiff responded to the pull on her collar and stopped. Her leash mates, Maggie and Jackson, both Malti-poos, stopped too. Gordon wound the leashes around a lamp post and picked up the cooling pile of canine excrement. He wondered how it had come to this. He'd put in over twenty-five years as a mailman and rarely missed a day of work. Now, thanks to the damn internet, he was permanently laid off. He was too old to start over and too young to get full retirement benefits. He'd been chased and bit by more dogs than he could count, and now he was a damn dog walker in a gentrified neighbourhood where there was more money than common sense. He slipped the poop bag over his hand, grabbed the gooey turd, gagged once, flipped the bag inside out, then tied a knot to keep it shut.

He'd dispose of the nasty package in a trash can in the park. Until then, he'd have to hold on to it. He bent over to untie the trio and was rewarded with a lick up the nose by Jackson. He stood and all three dogs perked up their ears and looked towards the bushes beside the sidewalk. Gordon punched the walk button and waited.

He saw a streak of black and a flash of bling as a cat sped past him. The dogs saw it, too, and before Gordon knew what was happening he was yanked off the sidewalk and into oncoming traffic.

"No!" he screamed as he heard the screech of tires. A blue Toyota Camry was headed straight for Gordon. He closed his eyes and threw his hands in front of his face. The dogs ripped free of his grasp and ran. He heard the ominous sound of the Toyota hitting a power pole, followed closely by the squealing tires of three more cars as they slid into each other.

Gordon opened his eyes. He was surrounded by cars and didn't have a scratch on him.

"Are you okay?" A woman rushed up and led him back to the sidewalk.

"I think so," Gordon said, feeling rather surreal. Then he smelled the distinct unholy fragrance of poop. He looked down. He had dropped the bag of doggy do and stepped in it, spreading the putrid shit all over the road.

"Oh no!" he cried. "The dogs! Where are the dogs!" He caught the briefest glimpse of the trio. They were a block up, across the street, and heading into the park.

"Damn it!" He turned to the woman. "I'm fine, I have to go!"

Gordon took off at a fast trot. He had to find those dogs. He thought about how he would explain this to the owners if he didn't find them. They had no children, were filthy rich, and the dogs were spoiled rotten. They had gone away for a romantic weekend and Gordon was charged with looking after their babies and their house while they were away.

He ran as best he could and when he got to the corner he hit the walk button to cross over to the park. Nothing happened. All the lights were out. Of course, the power pole, the damn power was out. Gordon gauged the flow of traffic and was about to cross when the black cat came scooting past him and disappeared up a side alley. Gordon watched as Bonita bound out of the park and into the snarl of automobiles.

"Stop Bonita! Stop!" he shouted and waved his arms as the mastiff ran past him. Gordon tried to step on her leash, but instead of stopping the dog, he was flipped onto his behind. Horns honked and people hollered as Maggie and Jackson followed in hot pursuit, their ears flapping in the wind. More vehicles collided like dominoes as he grabbed Jackson's leash. The poor dog choked as the collar grabbed his throat. By the time Gordon was upright and back on the sidewalk, the other two were gone.

Jackson coughed and looked accusingly at Gordon.

"Shake it off, Jackie. We have to find that cat!" Jackson's

ears perked up and he took off running with Gordon right behind him. When they reached the alley, Jackson stopped and sniffed the air. Nothing. He walked over to a fence. Nope, not here. He zigged and zagged up and down the alley frantically searching until he finally found what he was looking for. He looked up at Gordon, walked in a tight circle three times, and pooped.

"You've got to be kidding me!" Gordon reached into his jacket for a poop bag. "I hate this job and I hate picking up poop." Jackson watched him as he scooped up the poop, tied the bag shut, and tossed it in a nearby trash can.

A cacophony of sirens, honking horns, and people shouting filled the air as Gordon scoured the alley for the dogs. "Bonita! Maggie!" he shouted. It was no use. He couldn't compete with sirens and horns. He turned and saw a flash of black run from a yard, dart across the alley, and leap over a wooden slat fence. Bonita and Maggie were right behind it. Bonita easily cleared the four-foot fence, her leash trailing behind her. Maggie paced the fence, found an opening, and disappeared before Gordon could stop her.

"Seriously!" Gordon screamed. He picked up Jackson, tucked him into his jacket, and clamoured over the fence. There was more honking and swearing as the cat and dogs raced through the already snarled traffic and back into the park.

"Bonita! Maggie! Get back here!" Gordon yelled as he

chased after them. Once in the park he stopped and put Jackson on the ground. "Go find 'em boy. Let's get those girls." Jackson barked and took off after his housemates. Gordon and Jackson spotted them at the same time. They were in the middle of a foot bridge that went across a stream in the park. The cat was perched on the railing of the bridge, hissing, while the dogs snapped and barked at it.

"That's enough!" Gordon shouted as he approached the dogs, only half expecting them to listen. He wondered if he'd be charged with causing all those accidents. He couldn't afford a fine, let alone pay any damages. Jackson whined and pulled harder on his leash as Bonita lunged at the cat. The shiny cat collar caught on her rather formidable canine teeth and when she jerked backwards, she yanked the cat onto the bridge deck. Bonita stared at the cat and spat out a small piece of collar. Maggie was on the cat in an instant. She was a good little hunter and went straight for the throat. The cat hissed and growled, teeth and claws flashing as Maggie snapped and snarled. One moment there was yowling and barking, and the next was the sound of a cat hitting the water below. Maggie picked up the now tattered collar and shook it in victory. Bits of shiny stones bounced off the bridge deck. Bonita grabbed the other end of the collar. Jackson jumped in to help Maggie in a friendly game of tug-o-war. As the three fought over their trophy,

Gordon snatched up their leashes. When he next looked at the trio, they were all sitting nicely and licking their lips. Except for a few shiny stones on the ground, there was no trace of the collar.

"Time to get you home." He sighed as they walked back the way they came.

"That's him!" It was the woman who had helped him. "That's him, Officer. That's the man who caused the accident."

"You there!" the officer shouted. "Stay right there. We need to talk to you."

"Oh, hell no," Gordon grumbled. "Not today." Gordon pretended not to hear him and walked quickly back into the park. He'd seen a pathway by the creek, and he was certain he could find somewhere to hide down there.

"Stop! Police!" the officer yelled. "We need to talk to you, sir." Gordon broke into a jog. This of course pleased the dogs to no end. They happily ran in front, pulling him along. Gordon saw the creek just below the embankment, but where was the damn path? It was hard to believe that not long ago he was running from dogs. Now he was in cahoots with them and running from cops.

Gordon grabbed the leashes with both hands and tried to steer the dogs away from the edge of the ridge. The toe of his left shoe snagged on a barely visible tree root and in the next instant he found himself face first on the ground.

He spat out a mouthful of grass. The dogs, sensing less pull on their leashes, ran harder, pulling Gordon behind them.

"Stop!" he shouted just before the animals pulled him over the ledge. He tumbled ass over teakettle, his arms, legs, belly, back, butt, and head assaulted by twigs, brambles, and the odd small stone. Bonita yelped as he crashed into her at the bottom of the embankment. Maggie and Jackson jumped out of the way and then rushed to Bonita's side, licking her face and wagging their tails. Bonita stood and shook it off. All three dogs then sat and looked at Gordon as if to say, "That was great, now what?"

"Now we go home," Gordon said.

They'd only taken a few steps when Maggie whined and pulled towards the bushes. "Not you too?" Gordon reached into his pocket and grabbed a poop bag. "Fine, go ahead." He switched her leash to his right hand and let her go into the bushes. Jackson and Bonita waited patiently for her to do her business. A few seconds later she came out, tail held high. Gordon debated about picking it up, then transferred her leash into his left hand with the others and stepped into the bush to find her droppings. He picked up the tiny poop, tied the bag, and gingerly placed it into his pocket. Gordon's rotator cuff burned as Bonita gave the leash another tug.

"Enough," he hissed.

Over in the creek, something caught Gordon's eye. It

was the black cat struggling in the creek. It was frantically paddling and getting nowhere.

"Shit." Gordon looked around. The park and the path were empty. Everyone was gawking at the accidents. "Shit! Shit! Shit!" he repeated as he watched the cat go under. "Damn, it! Aw shit!"

Gordon ran up the path, dogs in tow. He reached a spot where the creek narrowed and he waded in. "Damn, damn it, damn it all!" he cursed as the cold water slapped against his man parts, causing them to instantly retreat into his body. All three dogs sat and watched from the edge of creek. Gordon, arms outstretched, took another step and the dogs pulled back on their leashes. "That's it," he encouraged them. "Hold tight." The water pushed against his legs and buttocks, putting him off balance. Bonita, Maggie, and Jackson held their ground.

There was the cat, barely moving his paws and heading straight for Gordon. He had one chance to save him and it had better work. Gordon reached out and snagged the cat by his back leg. The cat went under, emerging seconds later sputtering and yowling. Gordon grabbed it by the scruff, tossed it into his open jacket, then zipped it up tight as he waded to shore.

No one paid attention as he limped along clutching his stomach as his canine companions led the way home. Gordon stopped a block from where he was housesitting and opened the jacket to check on the cat. The black fury hissed and spat when Gordon tried to touch him. Then the cat used Gordon's belly as a springboard, leapt from the jacket, and sped off down the street. The dogs watched it go. It was time for dinner, not time for chasing cats.

Back at the house, Gordon unclipped their leashes, changed into dry clothes, and fed the dogs. Within minutes they'd gobbled their food and were fast asleep.

The next morning Gordon let the dogs outside in the spacious back yard. He wasn't going to risk someone recognising him on a walk. All he wanted to do was get this job over with and find another way to supplement his retirement. He retrieved the morning paper off the front porch and took it inside to read with his morning coffee. The accident had made the front page. Eight cars damaged in total, two taken to hospital for minor injuries, and the power had been out for three hours. Police were looking for a person of interest who had been walking a dog when the accident happened.

"One dog?" Gordon shook his head and took a sip of coffee. "So much for eyewitnesses," he said to himself. He flipped open the paper and there was a photo of a cat. The same damn cat that had caused all of this. He knew it was the same cat because of the stupid shiny collar. He read the headline.

Runaway Cat Returns Home Without $1M Collar

Gordon spat out a mouthful of coffee. It couldn't be? Could it? He continued to read.

Morgana Heinrich's cat, Simon, snuck out of his home yesterday afternoon wearing a diamond studded collar worth over $1 million dollars. Heinrich discovered the cat was missing and immediately called police, who were busy with an eight-car pileup only blocks away. A source close to the family said when the cat returned a few hours later it was wet, missing large chunks of fur from around its neck, and the collar was gone. Five of the smaller diamonds were recovered at a foot bridge in the park across the street from the accident. Police are asking for witnesses to come forward with any information about the missing collar.

Gordon shook his head, got up and put the newspaper in the recycle bin. He looked out the back door and noticed the sun reflecting off something shiny in a rather large human sized turd on the sidewalk. Over in the corner of the yard Maggie made her way out of the bushes while Jackson turned around three times, ready for his morning elimination. Gordon smiled and grabbed the poop bags. Perhaps he'd found a way to supplement his retirement after all.

The Last Jump

Michael walked across the field towards his helicopter. There were paper cups and Miss Saigon playbills everywhere; leftovers from yesterday's theatre in the park. He inspected the exterior of his chopper, then positioned himself in the pilot's seat and went over his checklist. He had a husband and wife booked for a 10 a.m. sightseeing tour. He glanced at his watch: 9:40 a.m.

In the parking lot, a man had strapped on a backpack and now jogged towards the helicopter. Michael went back to his pre-flight check. Moments later he looked up as the man climbed into seat beside him. He pushed a button and the blades whirred into action.

"You my 10 a.m.?" Michael asked.

"I sure am." the man replied, "The name's James."

"Where's your wife?" Michael handed James a headset.

"Just me," James said.

"Nice backpack." Michael smiled and showed James how to adjust the headset. Then he prepared for take-off.

James blew into his headset mic and was rewarded with intermittent static bursts. He ignored them, clicked on his seat belt and gave a thumbs up. He was about to do his hundredth jump. After this, he'd hang up his parachute.

Michael maneuvered the controls and the helicopter lifted off. Some of the playbills fluttered upwards and one flew into the open side of the helicopter. James picked it up, read it, and tucked it under his leg. "The story of love gone wrong," he commented as the helicopter flew away from the field.

Michael frowned as he heard static and James cutting in and out. Hopefully it would clear up or he'd have to land and fix it. "Love ... wrong," was all Michael heard. He turned and gave James a weak smile. He felt sorry for the guy, sightseeing all by himself. He wondered where his wife was.

Confused by Michael's response, James tried to elaborate. "You know, the suicide at the end of Miss Saigon. It was a sad ending." Then he changed the subject. "So how high are we flying today?"

" ... Suicide ... end ... sad ... how high," was what Michael heard through his head set. He really had to get them fixed. Was this guy talking suicide? He answered James's question.

"We'll level off at 5,500 feet." He glanced over at his passenger. The guy didn't look depressed.

James smiled as he heard " ... 5,500 feet." It was a great altitude for a chopper jump. He looked down and watched a river snake its way through ranchland and disappear into a forest. It was the perfect spot for his hundredth jump.

"I promised my wife this would be my last jump," he said into his headset. "It's time to say goodbye to skydiving."

"... wife ... jump ... goodbye," came crackling through Michael's headset. Maybe the guy was depressed. Michael worked the controls, levelled off and kept the helicopter in a stationary position.

"Listen buddy, I'm really not comfortable with you talking about jumping. How about we head back now." Michael tapped James on the shoulder to make sure he heard him.

"... you ... jumping ... now ..." was what James heard. This was it. He unbuckled his seatbelt and edged his way towards the open side of the chopper.

"Wait!" Michael grabbed James by the arm. "You don't have to do this!"

"You ... do this!" came crackling through the headset.

James double-checked the straps on his parachute. "Okay, let me go, I'm ready."

Michael held on tight to the man's arm as the words "let ... go." crackled in his ears.

"No!" Michael grabbed the man's backpack and pulled him back onto his seat. The helicopter wobbled slightly. Michael pressed a button and radioed a distress signal.

"Pan pan, pan pan, pan pan, helicopter alpha, tango, Romeo, yankee, passenger suicidal, very urgent. Do you read me? Over." The reply was pure static. He had to land right now. He checked his grip on the backpack and headed towards the landing field.

James stared in disbelief. This maniac was trying to rip off his parachute! Through the headset James heard, "fan ... dango ... very ... me" What the hell? Was this guy reciting the lyrics to *Bohemian Rhapsody*? At least he had his parachute, but that wouldn't do him any good if this nutcase crashed the helicopter.

"Let me go!" he hollered as he tried to pull away from Michael's grip.

"... will not let you go!" Michael screamed.

"Let me go!" James shouted again as Michael held tight to the backpack.

"... will not let you go," came crackling back at him. The ground was coming up fast. The guy was most definitely reciting *Bohemian Rhapsody*.

"Please, my wife loves me. Leave me alone," James begged. "I don't want to die. You can't do this to me. She's going to have our baby?"

Michael heard James's words crackling through the headset, "... love me ... leave me ... to die ... can't do this to me ... baby." What the hell? This guy sounded like he was reciting lines from *Bohemian Rhapsody*.

James broke free of Michael's grip just as the helicopter touched down. He tumbled out onto the ground as Michael cut the engine and the blades slowed and stopped. A couple ran across the field to greet them.

"Hi!" they shouted. "We're the Taylors. I believe we

have a 10 a.m. tour booked with you."

"Do *not* get in that helicopter," James shouted. "That man is completely insane. He tried to kill me while reciting Queen lyrics!"

"Me? Crazy?" Michael came around and squared off in front of James. "You were reciting *Bohemian Rhapsody* and tried to jump from my helicopter. You could have been killed!"

"That's why I was wearing a parachute, you idiot!" James pulled off the chute and waved it in Michael's face.

"Now it makes sense," Mr. Taylor said. "The pilot in the helicopter over there was expecting us to skydive."

Michael and James looked across the field and saw the other helicopter. The reality of the situation hit them.

"Uhhhh, ummm," Michael stuttered.

"Yah, uhhhh, I've had enough flying for today," James said as he walked back to his car. Ninety-nine jumps were enough.

Reap What You Sew

Sean Lundquist looked up as a black sedan rounded the corner and screeched to a halt. A woman got out, and the car sped away. She limped towards Sean and stared at him through red-rimmed eyes as she wiped a drop of blood from the corner of her mouth.

"Are you my eight p.m. fitting?" she asked and headed towards a doorway.

"Ahhh, I think so." He ran his fingers through his greying hair. "Ummm, are you Damaris Smirnov, the tailor?"

"Well, I'm not Santa Claus," she said as she punched a code into an entry keypad. The door swung open and interior lights came on. "Come in." She grabbed a suit from the front rack. "Go into the change room and put this on."

Sean entered the change room and Damaris disappeared into a back room. Moments later they both emerged; Sean in his new, somewhat ill-fitting suit, Damaris in a clean shirt and pants.

"Thank you for seeing me so late. I just found out my best friend is eloping, and they want me there tomorrow."

"Uh huh." She motioned for him to step up onto a round platform.

"You know," he said as she unceremoniously jabbed the measuring tape into his groin. "I was expecting a man."

"Really?" She hemmed the pant leg with pins.

"I meant no disrespect," Sean said, trying to ignore the swelling around her lip.

"Damaris is a girl's name." She repositioned herself in front of his other leg.

"It's nice," he said. "What does it mean?"

"Gentle," she said, as she jammed the measuring tape high into his inner thigh.

Sean winced, "Oh," he said, swallowing hard.

She hemmed the other pant leg and stood. "Arms straight out," she commanded.

He complied and raised his arms while she measured.

He felt braver now that she'd moved away from his dangly bits. "Ummmm, earlier ... the bloody lip thing ... Are you okay?"

Damaris sighed as she pinned his left jacket cuff. "Yeah, I wondered if you were going to ask about that."

"I, it's just that, well, you look like you're hurt."

"Arms down," she said as she placed the last pin in the other cuff. "Take it off and I'll hem it for you."

Sean went into the change room and returned wearing his own clothes. He handed her the suit. "Do you want to talk about it?" he asked.

"Follow me," she said and walked into the back workshop. "Sit there." She pointed to a wooden chair and took out her needles and threads. "It's my dad's fault," she said matter of factly. "For some reason, people think he was a Russian spy."

"A spy?" Sean leaned forward in his chair. "Really? Well, was he?"

"He was a tailor," she said. "Maybe he was a spy. I don't know." She expertly completed the hem on the first leg. "Now he's dead and they think I know things."

"Who are they?" Sean asked.

"The CIA, MI6, or Mossad, maybe all of them. Your guess is as good as mine. They think I'm a double or triple agent, or something." She grabbed a tissue off the table and wiped a fresh drop of blood from her lip.

"You mean like in *Tinker, Tailor, Soldier, Spy?*" Sean asked.

"Yeah, but I liked the book version better." She smiled and Sean couldn't help but feel a bit sorry for her.

"I guess you'd be Tailor then." He smiled at his own joke.

She scowled. "Tailor was the mole in that story." She finished up the second pantleg and moved on to the jacket. She skillfully snipped and folded the existing cuffs and then stabbed her needle into the material.

"Hmmm, true," Sean said. The pair fell silent for some time as her needle and thread quietly transformed the suit jacket.

Sean broke the silence. "Are you?" he asked as he fidgeted with something in his jacket pocket.

"Am I what?" Damaris began to hem the second cuff.

"A mole," he said.

She ignored him and finished sewing. She gave the jacket a quick shake and brought the suit over to the steam press.

"Why did you hand stitch it?" Sean asked. "You have an industrial machine right there."

"Broken pulley," Damaris replied over the hiss of the steamer. She pressed the suit and put it on a hanger. "This here." She reached into a drawer and pulled out a broken 3.5" metal pulley casing.

"Be careful," Sean said. "That edge looks sharp. You could cut yourself."

"You're right," she said as she handed Sean the suit, the broken casing still in her right hand.

"Oh?" Sean said.

"I'm just like Tailor." Her right hand slashed at his neck with the jagged edge of the pulley.

Sean was faster than he looked. He dropped the suit and rotated away from her. She screamed and lashed out at him again. He stepped back, but not soon enough. He felt a small trickle of blood on the back of his neck. He turned to face her as she kicked his feet out from underneath him. He fell with a thud against the steam press.

Damaris pounced on him, the broken pulley raised, ready to strike. Sean pulled a syringe out of his pocket and deftly plunged it into her shoulder. Her arm went limp and her eyes opened wide. Sean lifted her off him and sat her up against a wall. He brushed some thread ends off his trousers. He cocked his head and watched as her body deflated like an old blow up punching clown.

Her eyes glazed over. "Who are you?" she croaked.

"I'm Sean, remember? I have a wedding tomorrow." He picked up the suit off the floor. Damaris's eyes became unfocused and then closed. "Oh, and they call me, the soldier," he said. Then he turned and left the shop.

Inline Research

Kelsey grabbed a plastic bag from the grocery store stand and filled it with Ambrosia apples. "I don't see why you're so upset Matt. It's not like it's a pop quiz or anything. It's two short reports."

Matt took the apples from her and put them into the shopping cart. "They aren't short reports," he countered. "I have two papers due, one on consumer attitudes about food and one on mob mentality. That calls for research Kelsey, and you do research on the computer."

Kelsey laughed. "Yeah, so what?" She grabbed a head of romaine lettuce, popped it into a plastic bag, and handed it to Matt.

"It sucks me in! That's what," said Matt. "One minute I'm researching perceptions and changing attitudes towards our food and the next I'm on Facebook, then I click on a video and then I spend an hour researching and watching the world's best zit pops."

"Ewwwww!" Kelsey swatted him on the arm. "Gawd, you are so gross sometimes."

The pair slowed as they walked by the meat coolers. Kelsey picked up a package of bacon and put it in the basket. Matt grabbed package of pork chops and hesitated. "I saw a video on YouTube yesterday about a pig slaughterhouse. Now that, was gross." He put the chops down and headed towards the check out.

All the lines were full, including the double row of self-serve machines, but they still looked to be the fastest of the bunch. Shopping after school was always a bad choice. Matt scanned the line-up. There were a couple senior citizens, a few college kids, three moms, all with kids, and a tired-looking truck driver. Matt smiled at a little girl to his right as she carefully waved a package over the self-serve scanner. She was rewarded with a beep, and looked around to see if anyone had noticed that she'd done it right. Matt smiled and gave her a thumbs-up.

Kelsey poked Matt in the ribs. "Hey, why'd you put the pork chops back and not the bacon?"

"It was that slaughterhouse video I watched. It was so gross. I can't eat pork chops tonight." A teenage boy to his left turned around. "Yeah, I saw that too. How freaked out were those pigs! I'm never eating meat again."

Matt grinned at Kelsey. "See, it was gross."

"Hey, genius," Kelsey said, waving the package of bacon in front of his face. "You have to kill a pig to get bacon, but you kept that."

The little girl on their rightstopped what she was doing, stared at Kelsey and then her mother. "Mommy, do they have to kill pigs to make bacon?"

The mother froze and knelt down in front of her child. "Where'd you hear that, honey?" The little girl pointed towards Kelsey and Matt.

"How dare you!" The woman was in front of the pair in a heartbeat. "What gives you the right to tell my child where bacon comes from!"

The teenage boy chimed in. "What gives you the right to lie to your kid? How come she doesn't already know meat is dead animals?"

The little girl looked confused. "Mommy, did someone eat Lucky when she died?"

The mother wheeled back to her girl and put her hands on her shoulders. "Oh, no honey, we buried Lucky out by the rosebush. No one ate her."

A wispy haired grandpa at the far end of the self-serve line finished packaging up his purchases and came over to the little girl. He smiled and nodded to the mom and bent down to the girl's height. "When I was about your age, I had a pet pig named Wilbur. One day he was just gone and two days later my dad came home with enough meat to keep us fed all winter. It broke my heart when I found out the meat was Wilbur. But I gotta tell ya, he sure was tasty." He straightened up, ruffled the little girl's hair, and turned to leave.

"Wait just one damn minute!" the woman shouted. "Do you think that was supposed to help her? Now you've traumatized my daughter!"

A stocky, middle-aged woman pushed past Kelsey and

Matt. "Hey, that lovely gentleman is a neighbour of mine. You can't talk to him like that. He went to war to fight for our rights, including freedom of speech. He was only trying to make her feel better. I bet you're the kind of mother who won't tell her kid where food comes from and yet you let her watch Bambi." The woman turned to the girl. "Does your mom let you watch shows like Bambi?" The little girl nodded. The woman gave the mother her best I knew it smirk and stepped aside to let Kelsey and Matt go to a recently vacated self-serve check out.

Fuming, the mother abandoned her purchases, grabbed her purse and her daughter and tried to run out of the store. In her rush to leave, she bumped into the old man, who fell against the truck driver, who dropped his bag, spilling its contents onto the floor.

"Hey! Are you crazy! Watch where you're going, lady! I hope you drive better than you walk!" He steadied the old man and bent over to pick up his groceries as the woman fled with her daughter. "Women!"

He stood up just as a mother of twin boys stepped up and poked him in the chest. "I am so sick and tired of guys like you thinking you can put everyone in neat little groups to make your world easier to understand." He took a step back, slipped on a lime and fell to the floor.

"Manager! We need a manager over here!" cried one of the neighbouring cashiers.

The teenager, his purchases now complete, shouted out, "Clean up on aisle five!"

A college girl shook her head and rolled her eyes. "Boys," she said with as much disdain as she could muster.

"Oh yeah?" The teenager turned around and walked up to her. "I'm more man than you could handle," he snorted and walked away. "Screw you, bitch."

"No, screw you!" she screamed as she pelted him with a head of iceberg lettuce. The teenager tottered, but he did not fall. He rummaged through his bag, found a frozen pizza and tossed it at her like a Frisbee. She ducked.

"Hey!" screamed the store manager as the pizza hit him squarely in the chest.

"Food fight!" yelled one of the twins as he opened a carton of eggs and threw it at the neighbouring cashier. The egg hit her squarely in the back of the head. She grabbed some tomatoes off the conveyor belt and chucked them at the boys.

"How dare you!" screamed their mother. She reached into her shopping bag, ripped open a bag of bulk mixed nuts, and bombarded the cashier with them.

The truck driver, still on the floor, crawled behind a cash register. A freshly baked chicken potpie hit the counter, broke open and splattered all over the floor.

Kelsey grabbed Matt by the shirtsleeve. "Let's get out of here!"

"I haven't paid for the bacon yet!" he hollered above the dozens of screaming shoppers as a pomegranate whizzed past his head.

"Meat is murder!" screamed the teenage boy who was thoroughly enjoying the free-for-all.

"Leave it!" Kelsey grabbed the bags and Matt quickly punched in the PIN number for his credit card. "Hurry!" She was tugging at his shirt when a container of Greek salad, minus the lid, hit her square in the chest. "Jeezus, Matt, let's get out of here!"

Matt retrieved his card, grabbed the receipt, and tried to shield Kelsey from flying eggs as they made their way to the exit. They took one last glance at the melee behind them. The twins had graduated to peeling and throwing both the bananas and the peels; the teenage boy and the college girl took cover on opposite sides of the checkouts and were throwing chocolate bars at each other. The twins' mother continued her assault by opening a bag of frozen peas, and the truck driver retaliated with lunchmeat and buns. The old man sat on the bench and shook his head.

Kelsey and Matt bolted towards their car and pulled out of the parking lot as the police arrived.

"Wow," said Kelsey. "What the hell was that?"

"That," laughed Matt, "was all the research I need for my papers, and we did it inline, not online."

Deer God

The day did not start out well for Laurie. She had to work the afternoon shift and her daughter was home from school with a bad cold. Laurie's husband, Martin, promised he'd be home by noon, in plenty of time for her to get to work. She listened to the radio as she made some chicken soup for later. A local news reporter was telling a sad tale of a missing plane which held three local men. At the moment they were considered missing and a search team had been sent to the general area where they thought the plane might be.

Martin came home promptly at noon. His face was ashen. "Did you hear?" he asked as he hung up his coat and took off his shoes. "It was Sam, his brother and his nephew on that plane."

"What?" Laurie felt her knees go weak. "No, it couldn't be, we just saw him yesterday." Martin leaned in to hug her, but she pulled away. "I don't believe you." She went to her computer and pulled up the local online news. It was true. "Damn it!" she hollered and slammed her hand down on the desk. This was not good.

Laurie checked in on her daughter, held her husband tight, then dialed their friend. "Oh Jenny, I'm so sorry to hear about Sam. We are thinking of you and praying for them." The conversation was short, there was too much shock and disbelief to be put into words.

"There's soup on the stove for when she wakes up," Laurie said as she put on her coat. I'll be home around midnight." With that she headed off to work.

The rest of her shift went by without any news on the missing plane. Her grief covered her like a fever, making her wonder if she, too, was coming down with something. Finally, her shift was over, and she headed home.

As she turned onto the highway, she couldn't help but notice how clear the night was. Stars twinkled everywhere and aside from the sound of the engine, there was absolute silence.

She thought of Sam and the other men. "Are you out there? Are you okay?" she whispered aloud into the night.

An answer came back. "I'm okay."

That voice, his voice, laced with underlying laughter and good humour. It was him, loud and clear. He was either okay, or her imagination willed him to be that way.

"Oh gawd, I'm losing it," she said to no one in particular. "Well, since I'm talking to myself and hearing voices, I might as well ask another question. I believe you are okay, but are you alive?"

The air around her was silent. The dashboard lights cast an eerie green hue on her hands as she clutched the wheel.

She waited and then she heard the voice again, clear and strong.

"You ask too many questions. Go home." Again that unmistakable undertone of good humour mixed with mischief.

She decided she really was losing it and yet she needed answers. "Sam? Is that you?"

She was greeted with silence. She felt an anger begin to bubble inside her. She shouted into the car. "Why him? He was a good man. I knew him. He wasn't just a news story. What about his wife? His kids? Do we have any right to hope?" So many unanswered questions.

Laurie began to sob. "You know what, God? It's just stupid. That's what it is you know, just stupid." God didn't answer.

"It's not fair." Her voice was getting louder and she was sobbing uncontrollably. "They could be anywhere, alone, hurt, and no one to help them. Damn you! It isn't fair! How could you let this happen?"

The more she ranted the more her emotions took over and soon she was screaming at the top of her lungs. "Life isn't fair!" she hollered into the darkness. "No one should be hurt and lost and alone." She listened for an answer. There was none. Her voice dropped to a whisper. "How can I believe you exist if you allow things like this to happen?" Then she fell silent.

A few more minutes and she'd be home, down the winding hill and over the bridge. Her face was still wet with tears and she made one final plea. "God, please tell me they didn't die alone. I couldn't stand knowing that. Please God, help me to understand."

Laurie slammed on her brakes as she rounded the corner, barely missing a fawn. She pulled over, put on her flashers, and went to see if she could help. The fawn struggled, pulling itself across the road with its front legs as its back legs dragged behind it. More cars were coming down the hill. She flagged one down.

"Can you help me?" she asked, pointing to the fawn. "We have to get her off the road."

The man parked and helped move the fawn to the shoulder.

"Can you call the police?" she asked. "I'll stay here with her and make sure she doesn't get out onto the road again. I can't stand the thought of her getting hit again. What if she causes an accident and someone is injured, or worse?"

The man nodded. "I can stay if you want to go."

"No," Laurie knelt beside the baby deer and stroked her head. "I need to do this, but thank you."

The man nodded again, returned to his car, and drove off.

Laurie looked more closely at the fawn. Her spots were almost faded, barely visible in the light of the headlights.

Her eyes were wide, fearful, pained. Laurie spoke to her softly. "It's okay." She repeated those words over and over again, trying to calm the fawn. "I'm here. You aren't alone." Her eyes closed as Laurie continued to stroke her head.

There wasn't much blood. Laurie felt a tingle of hope. Maybe she would be okay after all. Maybe the police would come and take her to an animal shelter and have her legs fixed. Maybe she had a dislocated hip, not a break. Maybe they would take her to a game farm to live out her life. Maybe.

Laurie shifted her position and sat down in the dirt beside the fawn. She lifted its head and put it on her thigh. The fawn sighed beneath Laurie's hand as she stroked her nose, her head, and neck. Then the fawn opened her eyes and looked directly into Laurie's.

"I know you hurt, and I know you're scared, but I'm not going anywhere. I'm not going to leave you." Laurie whispered those words over and over again. It was her mantra. "It's okay, I won't leave you." A small trickle of blood dribbled from the fawn's nose and onto Laurie's lap.

Laurie looked up at the star splattered sky and began to cry again.   "God, please let her live."

Finally, a policeman arrived. Laurie stayed seated as he approached. "I don't think it's that bad," she said hopefully. "Her front legs work just fine and there's hardly any blood." Laurie didn't tell him about the blood that had trickled out of the fawn's nose. She watched as the police officer took a deep breath.

He spoke softly and slowly. "She'll be in pain for the rest of her life if we try to save her, if we can save her. I'm sorry, but I've seen enough of these to know it's not good."

Laurie didn't want to hear any more. "Can't you just take her somewhere? Help her?"

"I'm afraid not," he said. "You may want to leave now."

His eyes were sad but determined. Laurie knew he hated this. Hated doing what was right. Hated ending the suffering. Hated being the one who had to take a life to ease the pain. He reached a hand down to help Laurie up.

She stood, then knelt back down on the gravel beside the injured fawn. "I'm so sorry." Laurie kissed the fawn on the forehead and stood. "Forgive me for leaving you." She couldn't look at the officer as she got to her feet. She swiped at the ever-running river of tears on her face. "Could you wait until I'm over the bridge?"

"Of course," he said and then headed back to his cruiser to get his rifle.

Laurie got into her car, turned off the four ways, and just sat there. She watched in the rear-view mirror as the officer came back with a rather large looking rifle. She pulled her gaze away, started the car, and pulled onto the road. Her eyes were drawn back to the mirror. He looked as forlorn as she felt, a silhouette in his own headlights. He waited, the gun held loosely at his side, watching the fawn, waiting for Laurie to go. She took a deep breath, rounded the bend and drove over the bridge. A few seconds later she heard a muffled sound that echoed throughout the valley. It was over.

A few minutes later she was safe at home. She went into her daughter's room and kissed her warm cheeks. As she climbed into her own bed she couldn't help thinking about the day's events. It had started out badly and ended just the same. Before she knew it, she was sobbing again. She felt her husband's hand on her shoulder, and she told him what had happened with the deer.

"It's okay, you did what you could," he said.

Laurie sat up in bed. "You don't understand. I couldn't do anything. I was there, but I couldn't do a damn thing except wait for someone to come along and kill her." Laurie continued to sob inconsolably. All her grief for the lost men, for her inability to do anything to assist or comfort their grieving families, and her inability to save a baby deer poured out of her and onto the bed sheets.

"At least you were there," her husband said quietly. "She didn't die alone." He held her as she continued to sob and finally fell asleep.

The next day Laurie awoke with a realization. Fate had placed her exactly where she needed to be. She had asked questions and was given a task. She asked for understanding and was given the honour of comforting a living creature in its last moments.

They found the plane later that week. There were no survivors. Life still wasn't fair; however, Laurie knew in her heart they did not die alone.

Half a Man

The phone woke George from his nap. He rolled over, holding his limp left arm with his good right arm. "Damn phones," he muttered. "Ruin a perfectly good nap every time. I was dreamin' about baseball."

George tucked his useless hand into his pocket and scooted to the edge of the bed. He grabbed his walker with his right hand and pushed himself to a standing position.

"George! Telephone." His wife's voice swooped down the hallway. "It's Melissa, something about the bathroom."

"Bring it to the living room. I'm on my way." He steadied himself and made his way down the hall. He cursed silently as his left leg dragged behind. He plopped down into his easy chair and took the phone from Mildred.

"What's wrong now?" he grumbled.

Melissa ignored her father's tone and launched into her speech. "Just the bathroom door Dad. Josh was swinging on it again. The hinges won't stay in the doorjamb anymore. I want to fix it before we come over for dinner tonight."

George coughed into the receiver. "What d'ya mean, you're coming over for dinner? For God's sake, Melly, you were here last weekend!"

"Oh Dad, stop complaining. You love it when Josh and Dave come over."

"Do not," he countered. "Now what's wrong with the

damn door?" George coughed again and tried to get into a comfortable position. "Damn leg," he muttered.

Melissa picked up where she'd left off. "Josh was swinging on it again."

"Damn kid needs his ass paddled. That's what he needs. You're too easy on him Melly. Now when I was a boy ..."

Melissa chimed in, "You got whipped every day and twice on Sunday, even if you didn't need it." George could hear the smile in her voice. "Now, about my door."

"Yeah, yeah, the damn door, damn kid. Broken again, is it? Both hinges or just the top?"

"Just the top one. The bottom one is okay. I can't decide if I should fill the top holes with wood glue or stuff wood splinters in and then screw the hinge back on."

"Do both, Melly. Use that No More Nails stuff I gave you. That'll hold until the little monster decides to play Tarzan in the house again."

George thought back to a year ago, before he became half a man. Back then he would walk over there and fix it himself. He missed being able to walk. He missed simple things like getting in the car and driving down to the local coffee shop. He missed spending time with the other retired fogies. He missed going to their shops and puttering.

Ben had a welding shop that was always good for an afternoon of fixing yard tools. Old Casey had the best damn woodworking shop in town. Bob's shop was warm and dark and smelled of yeast. He made the best homemade beer around. His whiskey was pretty damn fine too. George hadn't visited the shops since his stroke.

"Do both?" Melissa interrupted his thoughts.

"Hell yes, do both. Fill the damn screw holes with the No More Nails and shove a few broken up toothpicks in and wait until it's dry. Then put the damn door hinge back on." George shook his head. He was surprised she didn't ask him to fix it for her. They used to ask him to come and do it, but that was before.

"Dad?" Melissa paused. "Are you okay?"

"Okay? Damn it, child, what do you expect? A man tries to have an afternoon nap and his 40-year-old kid wakes him up!" George coughed again.

"Sorry, Dad." She didn't sound sorry, though. She sounded just like she did the last 5,829 times she'd asked for help. Damn kids. Sure, it all starts out innocent enough. First you change their diapers, you help tie their shoes, teach 'em how ride a bike, and then it's help with the homework. Before you know it, you're teaching them how to drive, fixing flat tires, rebuilding motors and then renovating their house. Why, just three years ago he'd helped his son Mark and his wife add on another bedroom. Eight damn kids they had. Eight of them! He'd had pet rabbits with less ambition. Visiting them was a nightmare with eight little demons rushing madly about. Thankfully, they lived a few hours away. Melly, on the other hand, lived down the street. She only had one hellion to deal with. At least there was that. Her husband, Dave, was a good enough man, but he was a total waste of good tools.

Before the stroke, George and Dave had spent some time in George's shop. They'd built a few small things. A plant holder for Melly, a wooden spoon holder for Mildred, and a bike stand for Josh. That had taken all summer. Dave was more interested in philosophy and world events. George kept that kind of talk for his coffee crowd. His philosophy ran more along the lines of "spare the rod and spoil the child" and "guns don't kill people, people kill people." How the hell had he sired two namby-pamby small L liberals? It was beyond him. But he loved them.

"Okay, Dad, I'll do both. We should be over around six-ish. Tell Mom."

"Six-ish. What the hell is six-ish? You're going to be here around six, why can't you say that. What's with this fancy *isshhhh* crap?"

"I love you too, Dad. See you around six."

He hung up and set the phone on the arm of the chair. What did his kids expect of him now? He was paralyzed down one side. He couldn't really walk, let alone play golf, work in his shop, or drive a car. Mildred bought him one of those motorized old folks carts to drive around on. He took it out once and flipped it. He lay pinned beneath it on the side of the road for a half hour before someone helped him back up. He never rode it again. He hated being old and feeble.

George watched the early news and shut off the TV. He heard young Josh's exuberant shouts as he ran up the driveway, "Papa! Papa!"

George braced himself. What the hell was wrong with all of them? Didn't they realize he was half a man now? Only half his body worked, and the working parts didn't work that well either. Why did they act like nothing was different, when everything had changed?

Josh burst through the door, a fluorescent green Nerf ball in one hand and a toy fire truck in the other. "Catch, Papa!" Josh threw the ball straight at his grandfather's head. Without thinking, George raised his good arm and caught the ball before it had a chance to hit his nose. Damn kid! Why the hell was he throwing things at him?

George started to reprimand the child but stopped when Josh jumped on his lap, moved his limp arm out of the way and snuggled in for a hug.

"Great catch, Dad! You still have it in you." Melly planted a kiss on his forehead and headed for the kitchen. George rolled his eyes, shot a look after Melly, and pulled Josh in for a grandpa hug.

It wasn't Josh's fault. He was a good kid, and he was old enough to remember what it was like before. He remembered a grandpa that played catch. He remembered his Papa's tales of the good old days when he was a baseball star. He wished Josh could understand how different things were now. What had Melly said? He still had it in him? George was taken aback by the thought he could still have anything of his old self left in him.

Dave patted George on good his shoulder. "Thanks for giving Melly advice on the door. It's as good as new, for now. She inherited your talent for fixing things." Dave plopped down on the sofa. "Anything we can watch before dinner?" He picked up the remote and began to channel surf. Josh crawled off George's lap and played with his fire truck.

George opened his hand and let the Nerf ball expand to its full size. He stared at it and then at his grandson. None of them really treated him any different since his stroke. They still called for advice, woke him up from naps, and even tossed him a ball. They hadn't changed—he had.

Maybe he did still have it in him. He pulled back his good arm and pelted Josh in the forehead with the soft green ball.

"Catch, slugger!" George laughed as the ball bounced harmlessly off Josh's head. The boy whooped and ran after the ball. He picked it up, spun around, and threw it wildly at his Grandpa. George lunged to the right and caught the ball.

"Good catch, Papa!" Josh grinned at his grandfather.

George smiled. He could still catch a damn ball. Life wasn't so bad after all.

Her Breasts

They were not as they once were, but he loved them anyway. He sat on the edge of the bed and watched her through the crack in the bathroom door. She took her time undressing as she readied herself for her morning shower.

His eyes were on her breasts. They swayed ever so slightly as she moved. They were larger now, heavier than when he'd first noticed them four decades ago. They no longer pushed forward, taunting and proud. Now they sat lower, relaxed, comfortable.

He remembered the first day he saw her breasts. He was seventeen, in his last year of high school, full of bravado and about as wise as any teenager can be. He walked through the halls, bragging of his prowess with the young ladies. His friends laughed loudly, patted him on the back and urged him on. The first time he saw her, she was standing in profile beside her locker, much like he was seeing her now.

Her breasts were the first things he saw. He supposed that was how nature had intended it to be. They weren't large. No, quite the opposite was true. She was barely fourteen herself, past the halfway point of her bloom, long in the leg, thin but curved in the hips. What held his gaze were her breasts. They pushed at her sweater, not quite a woman's breast, no longer those of a child.

The first sight of her breasts changed his life. He once boasted he would never marry until he had travelled the world and bed a woman from every country. When he was old, at least twenty-nine, he would consider taking a wife.

The moment he saw those breasts, he knew that could no longer be. She turned her head slightly and looked at him. He sensed movement; his gaze slowly worked its way up from her breasts. His gaze was met by a pair of sky-blue eyes, framed by dark hair. Deep, penetrating eyes fringed by thick, dark lashes. They drew him away from the object of his desire, but only for a moment. He glanced back down at her breasts, then up again to her eyes.

He didn't notice his friends had walked away. He didn't notice that she stood beside him. Most of all, he didn't notice that he faced her, looking for all the world like young man who had been struck dumb. She spoke first. At least, he thought she did. From that moment on, he was lost to the rest of the world.

He remembered his graduation night. She wore a soft, pink sweater, her breasts a constant torture to him. He'd watched them ripen over the school year and he knew that if he did not touch them soon, he would surely go mad. He'd waited so long. She was a good girl in the ways of old movies and tales from family dinners about how it was in Grandma and Grandpa's day. His loins did not want her to be a good girl. The ache below was a constant companion, day and night. Until that night, she had never faltered.

She had three years left of high school. He was going away to university. She promised to write every day. He promised to be faithful. She believed him.

They said their goodbyes by the light of a quarter moon. He moaned and held her close, feeling her soft roundness resist beneath him. His hand went to her breast; she pushed it away. He sighed. Then she gently took his hand and guided it under the soft, pink sweater. It was the first of many gifts she would give him.

She kept her word and wrote every day. He kept his promise to be faithful. She graduated early and joined him at university during his third year. By mid-October, his desires burned hotter than ever. She was still a good girl, in all the ways that mattered. He phoned her father and asked his permission to marry her. They were married in late May and by September her breasts began to swell. Her belly followed suit.

He excelled in all his studies and was approached by one of the country's top companies to come and work for them. By the following June he had a new job and a new son. Life was good.

He recalled the first time he watched his son suckle on her breast. He was about to leave the room and give her privacy when she touched his arm and patted the bed beside her, bidding him to stay and share the moment. She opened her night-shirt, her dark hair falling down to the top of her magnificent breasts. His eyes marvelled at the creamy texture, following the curves of her breast until it dipped and met with the dark areolae and finally ended with the pink nub of her nipple. He watched as a tiny pink mouth rooted around and latched on. A flawless newborn cheek rested against his wife's flawless breast. Tears flowed freely as he paid homage with his eyes.

Time passed. Two more healthy children came into their lives and as with the first, he wept as he watched them nurse for the first time. He wept for the joy of another life he would help shape. He wept for his wife and her devotion. Mostly, he wept for the delicate beauty of her breasts.

He remembered how they felt, years later, no longer jaunty, but still incredibly soft, round and marvellous to touch. He remembered how they moved when they made love, how they felt, how they tasted. Time shuffled his memories and placed them into a collage. A momentous collage of her ever changing breasts.

More time passed; children grew. He watched as she held each one close to her breasts, giving comfort. He watched her face as one by one they withdrew from the comfort of her bosom to the uncertainty of the world.

He watched as they returned, wounded by one of life's unfair certainties, to the haven they'd always known.

Read My Shorts

He watched. He felt sadness and liberation as one by one his children made their way into the world as young adults. And still today ... he watched.

She stood naked, not knowing he was watching. She tested the shower water with her hand. He lazily let his eyes travel from breast to breast and finally up the curve of her neck to her face. His eyes naturally returned to where they belonged. These were the breasts of his life-long companion and friend; these were the breasts of his wife.

A small tear made its way down his cheek, slowed by the furrows and creases that time had bestowed upon him. He sighed and smiled as she stepped, out of sight, into the shower.

Mabel's Gentleman Caller

"Dang it, Lucas! Move!" Mabel Ogilvie almost tripped over her dog while carrying the serving platters across the kitchen. Lucas stopped his frantic pacing, looked at her forlornly, then hid under the kitchen table.

Ma was out front, tidying up. She'd polished their new oak dining table until it shone. Pa was in the barn tending to the livestock.

Mabel placed the platters beside the wood stove, then closed *Mrs. Beeton's Book of Household Management* and placed it on a kitchen shelf. She sighed. Most of her friends were married off by eighteen. She'd turned eighteen in March and it was already May. There was talk of her becoming an old maid. Now, she was about to have her first bona fide gentleman caller, and one she'd only met that morning!

Mabel's cheeks flushed as she remembered Gus's hands around her waist when she'd tripped on the sidewalk. His eyes were a warm, deep brown, and his skin so tanned one might think he was a coloured fellow. Maybe he was. She didn't care. She'd heard her Pa talking about how someone started the NAACP a few months earlier. He said it was about time. Every man ought to get paid proper for his work and be able to vote and own his own home. It didn't matter the colour of his skin. She hoped he wasn't just spoutin' off to impress her ma.

After her spill on the sidewalk, Gus took her into the General Store for a soda and to check her ankle. She'd got up the nerve to ask him over for dinner that night and he agreed. She floated home on possibilities.

When she reached the farmhouse, Mabel announced to her parents that she was making dinner for a gentleman caller. Then she marched out to the barn, found her least favourite hen, and chopped off its head. The bird was now roasting in the oven on a bed of potatoes, carrots and onions. Its feet, liver, heart, gizzards, and neck simmered away in a broth on the stove with some well-weathered turnips from the root cellar. She would add the bones into the broth after dinner.

Mabel opened the door to the oven and let the scent of freshly made spice pie and roast chicken envelop her. She hummed, "Cuddle up a Little Closer, Lovely Mine," and grabbed a thick pot holder from the counter. Her cheeks flushed again as she remembered how Gus's strong hand gently prodded at her ankle. The sight of him on one knee in front of her made her positively giddy!

There was a knock on the door as Mabel placed the pie on the counter to cool. "Ma, can you get that?" Mabel rushed to the wash basin, rinsed her hands, patted them dry on her apron and smoothed her hair. She started for the living room, then pulled off her apron and hung it on the back of the door. She took a deep breath, steadied herself, and walked out of the kitchen.

There he was, standing there as handsome as she remembered.

"Please, sit down." Mrs. Ogilvie gestured to a single straight back chair she'd pulled out from the dining table.

"Thank you, ma'am," Gus said as he lowered his lanky frame onto the chair.

Mrs. Ogilvie smiled and positioned herself on the overstuffed chesterfield across the room.

"Mabel tells me you saved her from a terrible tumble this morning, Mr ..." Mrs. Ogilvie's voice trailed off. Mabel hadn't told her Gus's last name. She wondered if the girl even knew it.

"It's Johnson, ma'am. Gus Johnson." He started to stand, and Mrs. Ogilvie motioned for him to stay seated.

"I'll get us some lemonade," Mabel said as she turned to go back into the kitchen. She hoped her ma liked him.

She stole another glance at Gus and could have sworn she felt the earth move when he smiled at her. She took another step and then pitched backwards onto the arm of the chesterfield. The ground beneath the house groaned and shuddered.

"Oh my good ... " A vase slipped off the side table and

crashed to the floor before she could finish.

Mrs. Ogilvie shrieked and tried to stand. "Oh my!" she managed to sputter, before she was tossed back onto the cushions.

"Ma!" Mabel screamed. The coat rack near the front door crashed to the ground. Pictures fell off the walls and dust and debris rained down upon them.

"Mabel!" Gus hollered above the roar. "Quick! Get under the table!" Mabel fell to her knees and crawled towards him. "Mrs. Ogilvie, take my hand!"

Mabel's mother reached for it, rolled off the chesterfield and fell to the floor. Gus grabbed her by the shoulders and unceremoniously shoved her under the dining table.

"Gus! Look out!" Mabel screamed. She grabbed his arm and pulled with all her might. The ceiling light fixture crashed down, right where Gus's head had been.

Mabel and Gus looked at each other in surprise, then belly crawled in unison to the safety of the table.

By the time Mr. Ogilvie made it to the house, the shaking had stopped. Mrs. Ogilvie wriggled out from under the table and ran into his arms. Mabel and Gus emerged a few seconds later, shocked, but unhurt.

Gus dusted off his hands and held one out to Mr. Ogilvie. "How'd you do, sir? I'm Gus, Gus Johnson," he said.

Mr. Ogilvie smiled and he shook the offered hand.

"Well," he said, "you sure know how to make a first impression."

Years later Mabel and Gus would tell the story of the first time they saved each other from harm's way. It was a Sunday, they'd say, May 16, 1909. The day of the Great Plains earthquake. The day they learned the hard way about the Hinsdale fault line along the Saskatchewan/Montana border. It was also the last day Mabel ever had to worry about being an old maid.

The Test

Jessie rushed into the unisex washroom at the resort, locked the door, and breathed a sigh of relief. There was nothing in the world as good as peeing when your bladder was ready to burst. She finished, washed and dried her hands, and tossed the paper towel into the full garbage can. It bounced off a white object and hit the floor. She picked up the towel, then used it to pick up the object. It was a pregnancy test, and it was positive. She put it back, thankful it wasn't hers.

Someone knocked on the door. "All done," she called and stepped out into the hallway. She couldn't believe her eyes. Standing before her was the man who had ghosted her.

"Andy, wow. So, you're still alive."

Andy heard the venom dripping from her words. "Jessie! Am I ever glad to see you! I lost your number. How are you?"

"Yeah, right," Jessie said. "Have a nice life." She turned and headed down the hallway. What were the odds of running into him here? Her stomach felt jittery, and her legs a little wobbly. But she wouldn't allow herself to still have feelings. He'd disappeared after a few dates and one amazing night at his place.

Andy watched her go and then entered the bathroom.

He'd thought about her every day for the past two months. He'd lost her number when he'd lost his phone. Unfortunately, he didn't know where she lived. They'd met at restaurants for their dates, and their last night together at his place was fantastic. The next day he lost his phone. He knew she was a bookkeeper but had no idea where. He'd called around with no luck. He'd returned to the deli where they'd first met, still no luck. And now, here she was.

Andy finished up, washed his hands, and threw the paper towel in the garbage. The pregnancy test caught his eye. He picked it up and looked at it. It was positive. Could it be? No wonder she was so mad at him. Could fate have brought them together at this mountain resort, to let him know she was pregnant? A thousand thoughts rushed through his head. He liked her and the time they'd spent together had been amazing. Was he ready to be a father? He stuffed the pregnancy test into his jacket pocket and headed for the hotel lobby. He'd searched the entire resort and was unsuccessful in getting her room number from the front desk. He went back to his room and packed. It was time to give up and go home. He grabbed his suitcase and headed to the gondola which would ferry him away from the resort and down to the parking lot. It arrived and three young men stepped off. Andy stepped inside and watched the gondola doors begin to close.

"Wait!" a woman called as she slipped inside.

"Oh, it's you," she said as she placed her suitcase on the floor.

"I've been looking all over for you," Andy said. Were her breasts larger? Yes, they looked larger. He heard that happened to pregnant women, even before they started showing in the belly area.

"Are you staring at my breasts?" Jessie asked. "Gawd, first you ghost me and now you stare at me like a piece of meat. You're such a jerk."

"No, no," Andy stuttered. "I mean, yes, I was, but ... "

"Where have you been for past last two months? I called you every day for three days. I thought we had something special." Jessie crossed her arms and looked out the window.

Andy sighed. "Look, I lost my phone, and I didn't have your number written down. How are you?" He looked at her arms crossed over her belly. "Do you feel sick? Can you feel it yet?"

"What?" Jessie turned to face him. "Feel what? Are you asking me if I still feel something for you? Leave me alone." Jessie wasn't about to let this schmuck know he still made her knees weak.

"But ... " Andy fumbled for the right words, then looked back at her breasts. Yes, they were definitely larger. He was sure of it.

"Stop looking at my breasts!" Jessie shot him a dirty look and pulled her jacket closer to her body.

"I can't get you out of my mind, Jessie, and now there's this." Andy pulled the pregnancy test out of his pocket.

Jessie stared at the plus sign on the stick. "Oh, so it was you. You got someone pregnant and now you're hitting on me! I was a fool for thinking we had something special. You're such a jerk."

"No, I'm not ... I mean, this ..."

"Just stop, Andy. A small part of me was hoping we'd get back together after seeing you today. But this ... this is low."

"How is this low? I want to see you again, to be with you!" Andy was confused. "Why is this wrong?"

"Let me see," Jessie was furious. "You knocked someone else up, then you see me and decide you want me back. Damn that's cold." Jessie turned away.

"What? No!" Andy waved the stick at Jessie. "I thought this was yours! You're the pregnant one."

Jessie gasped. "What? You think that's mine? Wait, you found that in the bathroom?"

"Yes," Andy said. "And I want to make it right. We had something, Jessie. I spent weeks looking for you!"

Jessie laughed. "No, that's not mine. It was in the bathroom when I got there."

"Oh, then, ummm." Andy's face turned red.

"Yah, so you're walking around with a stranger's pee stick in your pocket." Jessie laughed.

Andy stuffed the pregnancy test back in his pocket as the gondola reached the parking lot.

"So," Andy said as they stepped out of the cabin. "Can we try this again?"

Jessie hesitated. She wanted to believe him. "Ah, what the heck," she said as she dropped her suitcase, wrapped her arms around his neck, and answered him with a kiss.

BB and the Pig

Not long ago, in a land far away, folks readied themselves for the annual marathon. The prize was a huge pot of gold.

BB Wolf wanted that gold. He was tired of working hard and not getting anywhere. He blamed it on his parents. He blamed it on his boss. He blamed it on the queen, and he blamed it on the creatures he bullied.

"Name please," droned a tired looking dwarf.

"BB Wolf," BB said. "What time does the race start?"

"Tomorrow at 9:00 a.m." the dwarf said as he handed BB his number. "You're 191. Be at the park entrance at 8:30 a.m."

BB snatched the number down and stomped off. 191! He should have had a lower number. He was so upset; he didn't notice the little tin can sitting in front of a homeless pig on the sidewalk. BB kicked it and a few coins spilled out.

The little pig looked up, then quickly bowed his head. "Stupid pig," BB said. "Stop begging for money from hard working people. Go home or get a job!" His anger spent; BB walked away.

"Thanks to you I don't have a home anymore," whispered the pig as he gathered up his coins from the sidewalk. A tiny purple fairy watched him from an awning. She hated to see others suffer, but until a wish was made, there was nothing she could do.

It was getting late. The little pig gathered up his tin cup and headed towards the park. On the way, he stopped in front of a bakery and eyed the goodies in the window. The owner waved at him to come in.

"Hey Stanley, how was collecting today?" That's what the baker called it. He never called it begging.

"It was okay. I have five coins and a button." The little pig held up his tin can for the baker to see.

"That's a nice button. I lost one like that last week. Tell you what, Stanley, I'll trade you that button for some day-old corn bread. Deal?"

"Oh yes, that would be lovely," Stanley said. He shook the button out of the can and onto the counter. "You are too kind."

"You have a nice night, Stanley," the baker said. "Come by tomorrow and I'll give you a great deal on some day-old muffins."

"Okay," Stanley said. Cornbread in hand, he left the store and made his way to the far corner of the park. He'd made himself a twig shelter in the bushes by an old oak tree. So far, no one had bothered him there. He crawled in and laid out his meagre meal for the day. He ate slowly, savouring every bite. There was a rustling in the bushes and then a pink snout appeared.

"Hey, Stanley, how goes it?"

Stanley wiped crumbs from his chin and smiled. "Pretty good, Henry, how about you?" The visiting pig made himself comfortable.

"Good. The farmer and his wife have decided to hire me full time. My building skills with straw have impressed them so much they had me build three more little houses. I heard them talking about charging admission to see the little town built from straw."

Henry sniffed the air. "Cornbread?"

"Yah," Stanley said. "Sorry, I ate it all."

"Don't worry," Henry said. "They feed me at the farm. I just wanted to see how things were with you." He paused and looked around the tiny shelter. "Have you heard from Walter?"

"No, not since he kicked us out." Stanley sighed. "He's probably still living in his brick house in the woods."

"Ah, chin up kiddo. You'll get a job soon, then you'll have a real home again."

Stanley lit a small stub of a candle and placed it in the middle of the shelter. "I saw him today."

"Saw who?" Henry's ears perked up.

"Him." Stanley took a deep breath and let it out slowly. "Big Bad Wolf." He let his words leak out of the shelter and into the night.

"Holy moly!" Henry stood and paced the small space. He was careful not to singe his tail on the candle. "Did he recognize you? What did you do?"

"No, he didn't recognize me. He kicked over my tin can. I kept my head down. He's just as mean as ever."

The pair sat in the flickering light, each remembering the day the Big Bad Wolf had destroyed their homes.

"He had a big paper with a number on it. I think he's running in the marathon tomorrow," Stanley said. "I wish I had long legs like a giraffe. I'd run that marathon and I'd win."

Henry snorted and nodded. "You sure would, Stanley. Well, I've got to get back to the farm. Tomorrow I'm building a straw church for the tiny town square."

The pair said their goodbyes and Stanley blew out the candle. He curled into a corner and fell fast asleep.

The next morning, he awoke to the sound of children laughing. He'd slept in! He'd heard there was an opening at the furniture factory and he wanted to apply. Now it was too late. He needed to set up his collecting spot. Today was going to be a busy day with everyone coming to watch the marathon. He tried to stand and bumped his head.

"What the heck?" he squealed. His legs were spotted and oh so long. He belly-crawled out of the shelter, stood, got dizzy, and almost fell over.

"Good morning, Stanley," a cheerful voice called from

a tree branch. Stanley found himself face to face with the tiny, purple fairy. "You have no idea how long I've waited for you to make a wish. Do you like them?"

"What? I mean … how?" Stanley stared at her and then down at his giraffe legs.

"I'm a fairy, your fairy. You made a wish," the fairy said as if it was all rather normal and not at all bizarre to wake up one morning and be six feet taller than you were the night before.

"Wow," was all Stanley could say. Then he remembered his manners. "Thank you." He looked around in wonder at all the things that were now at eye level. "But why?"

"You wished for long legs. Voila, long legs." The fairy giggled. "I'm so glad you didn't wish to win the marathon. When too many people wish for the same thing, all the wishes go into a bucket and one gets drawn at random. This way you have a good chance." She clapped her hands and fluttered her wings. "Oh, I almost forgot. I registered you already. Here's your number. You have ten minutes to make it to the parking lot by the starting line." The fairy pulled a large shiny paper from behind the tree. It had the number 232 written on it in black ink. She fastened it around Stanley's neck. "Good luck!" And with that, she disappeared.

Stanley looked down at the number. He wasn't a runner; he was a builder. He might have the legs now, but he didn't have the lung capacity of a runner. Now, Big Bad Wolf, he had some amazing lungs.

The fairy appeared on the tip of his nose. "I almost forgot one important thing. Every time you doubt yourself, every time you don't believe you can win, your legs will get shorter. Now get out there and run!" And then she was gone.

"I can do this!" Stanley said. He turned and trotted towards the parking lot on the other side of the park. His new legs felt pretty good. He arrived at the parking lot at 8:26 a.m. and gathered with the other runners. There were at least 250 of them, all hoping to win the prize. He had never seen this many ordinary, mystical and magical four-legged creatures in one place before. They milled about, stretched their legs, ate protein bars, and drank water. Stanley hadn't had breakfast, but there was a water fountain nearby. He went over and took a long drink. "I can do this," he said to himself. "I can win this."

At 8:30 a.m. precisely, an official stepped up on the podium and spoke into a microphone.

"These are the official rules," barked the official. "Rule #1. No pushing or shoving. Anyone caught touching another runner with intent to harm or slow them down will be disqualified. Rule #2. Stay on the road. Anyone caught taking short cuts will be disqualified. Rule #3. You will line up at the start according your number, ten per row. Anyone caught ahead of the row they should be in, will be disqualified."

The crowd that gathered to watch the race had spilled out of the stands, off the sidewalks and onto the grass beyond. Stanley looked over to the stands and watched as the queen took her seat.

"Runners, take your places." The participants jogged to the start line, making sure they were in the right row. Stanley was near the back, so he took his time. He spotted BB Wolf slightly ahead of him. He wanted to hide behind someone, but he was too tall. Fortunately, the wolf never looked back.

Volunteers marked the front ankle of each runner with their number, making sure everyone was in the right place. By the time they got to Stanley he was quite nervous.

A troll wrote 232 on Stanley's ankle. "You're in the wrong spot," the troll said. Stanley began to panic. He couldn't be disqualified! "You're one row up," the troll said as he pointed to where Stanley should stand. Stanley smiled, nodded, and stood in his proper row.

At precisely 9:00 a.m., the announcer's voice boomed over the loudspeaker. "On your marks, get set, GO!"

Stanley easily passed the first twelve rows with his long stride, but he was feeling rather winded. He knew he had to slow down or he'd never finish the race. He concentrated on staying in the middle of the pack and thought about what he'd do if he won. With a huge pot of gold, he would never have to worry about food or shelter again. He could get a new home. He could help his homeless friends and he could pay the baker back. Stanley was jarred out of his daydream when a minotaur shoulder checked him into a bush. A course official zoomed onto the track, stopped the minotaur and disqualified him. Stanley shook the leaves off his snout and got back into the race.

"Oh wow," he said to himself. "Another hit like that and I'll never win." Stanley felt his knees buckle and realized he'd shrunk! His legs were now only five feet long. Still, he reminded himself, that was enough to win. He took a deep breath, thought about beating BB Wolf and charged ahead. By the time he was at the halfway mark he was up front with the top twenty runners. BB was just a few feet ahead.

A unicorn and a sphinx smiled at Stanley and wished him good luck as he ran past them. Now he was beside the wolf. Stanley's pace began to falter. What if the wolf recognized him? He wasn't sure if he could run past the wolf. Stanley started to doubt himself.

"Focus Stanley!" The fairy appeared in front of him, cheering him on. "You've got this."

Stanley took in a deep breath and pressed on past the wolf. He was now among the top ten runners with only a third of the way to go. His lungs burned and his new legs hurt, but he kept running.

"Here piggy, piggy."

Stanley turned. It was BB. The way he grinned at Stanley sent cold shivers down his spine. Stanley gave a little squeal as the wolf pulled up beside him.

"I recognize you. You're the twig builder aren't you. What's it like to be homeless?" The wolf laughed.

Stanley looked down as his legs wobbled and shrunk. That last bit of doubt had cost him dearly. His legs were now only three feet long, about the same as the wolf's.

"What delicious looking legs you have little pig," the wolf said, then he sprinted ahead of Stanley.

The fairy appeared beside Stanley's ear. "You've got this. You can have a home. Don't let that bully get to you. You can do this."

Stanley dug deep within himself. He could see the finish line ahead. Yes, he could do this. He needed to do this. He picked up the pace and with a burst of speed, ran past the wolf and two chimeras. He was now in fourth place. Just a little bit farther.

The crowd roared. The queen waved her arms and cheered as the runners made their way towards the finish line.

He was almost there. He was so close. He glanced to his right and saw BB pull up beside him.

"I'm going to get you after this, little pig," growled BB as he passed Stanley. The wolf was now in second place, right behind a centaur.

Stanley could see the blue ribbon of the finish line and he gave it one last try. His head pounded, his legs felt like Jell-O and his lungs were on fire. Just a little bit farther. His brow furrowed as he concentrated on every breath, every step. He pulled up beside the wolf. They were tied for second.

"You're going to be my dinner," sneered the wolf.

Stanley shuddered as his legs gave way. He was now back to his short-legged self. He didn't care. He ran as fast as his little piggy legs would carry him and passed the wolf.

"I can do this!" he shouted.

He heard the wolf growl and take a deep breath. There may have been a rule about touching another runner, but there were no rules against blowing them off course. Stanley was now neck and neck with the centaur.

"I can do this!" he shouted and leapt for the finish line just as the wolf expelled a huge blast of air. Stanley tumbled head over tail, just over the finish line. He had done it!

Stanley stood proud on the podium. He bowed his head as the Queen placed a medal around his neck and handed him his pot of gold. Stanley burst into a full body grin that wiggled its way through his belly and made his tail quiver. It was over. He'd won. He was tired, but happy. He now knew he could do anything, as long as he believed in himself. Now he could start over and live happily ever after.

Janai's Wishes

Not long ago, in a neighbourhood much like yours, was a little girl named Janai. She sat on a folding chair on the sidewalk, drawing. The crowd around her shouted encouragement to the runners as they passed by.

Every weekend was the same thing: drive to another city, stay with friends or relatives, and wait for her mom and dad to run by. She never got to see them. Janai's parents loved to run marathons and were either running, training, or visiting. She wished they would stay home. She wished they would stop running.

Janai would never be a marathon runner. She was different from the other kids. Her legs and arms were short, and her head was large. Sometimes the kids would call her pumpkin or bobble head. Some called her short stop and others asked her if she was cold down there. The rest of the time, they ignored her.

"Here they come, Janai!" Aunty Sandra shouted. She reached down and scooped Janai onto her shoulders so she could see above the crowd.

"Go Mommy! Go Daddy!" Janai waved her arms as her aunt struggled to keep her aloft.

The small group passed, and the crowd began to thin.

"Okay Janai, let's go to the car and head to the finish line." Aunty Sandra put her down on the sidewalk. "Pick up your pencils and paper and I'll get the chair."

Janai bent over to pick up her coloured pencils, but one escaped and rolled down the sidewalk. It stopped right under the foot of a sleeping woman leaning against a brick wall. A grumpy looking, wrinkled man sat beside her.

"Get out of here!" the old man hissed. "We don't want your kind around here."

Janai stepped back. She could just make out the tip of her pencil crayon. She took a deep breath and lightly touched the woman's foot.

"Excuse me," she said politely. "Can I get my pencil crayon please?"

The woman sat up, rubbed her eyes, and ran her fingers through her dirty blonde hair. She had the bluest eyes Janai had ever seen.

"I said get out of here!" The old man leaned closer to Janai. She could smell his putrid breath.

"What do you want?" the woman mumbled.

Janai pointed. "My pencil crayon. It's green. I dropped it and it went under your shoe."

The woman shifted and looked under one foot, then the other one.

"Here you go, kid." She handed over the green pencil. "My name is Nissa." She held out her hand.

Janai was about to shake it when the old man grabbed her wrist and leered at her. "Be careful short one, we eat folks like you for dinner you know."

"Janai! No!" her aunt screamed as she snatched her niece away from the grizzled man. She glared at them, turned and walked away with Janai in tow.

"He was weird, but she was nice," Janai said, struggling to keep up with her aunt. "She gave me back my pencil crayon." Janai held it up, but her aunt shook her head and made huffing noises until they arrived at the car.

"Get in."

Janai hopped into the back and climbed up on her booster seat.

"You shouldn't talk to strangers, especially homeless ones. It's dangerous. You don't know what they did to become homeless. It's best you ignore them."

Aunty Sandra started the car and drove the thirty blocks to the finish line at the city park.

"Leave your things here. We won't be long." She helped Janai out of the car.

The pair made their way through the park and found a spot close to the finish line.

"The runners should be coming around the corner any minute now," Aunty Sandra said as she scanned the horizon.

"Great," Janai said, but she didn't mean it. Soon they'd go back to Aunty Sandra's and talk about the race and Janai would be ignored. She looked around at the crowd, but all she could see were feet, ankles, and knees. She had to lean her head way back to see their faces.

"I wish I was super tall," she muttered to herself.

"Pssssst! Over here!"

Janai looked at all the faces. No one looked back.

"No, silly, down here."

Janai peeked through the sea of legs and saw Nissa leaning against a tree in the park behind them. She beckoned Janai to come closer. Aunty Sandra was still watching for the runners.

Janai made her way through the forest of knees and thighs until she broke into the wide-open space of the park. Nissa smiled and patted the ground beside her. Janai smiled back and sat down, their backs against an old oak tree.

"How'd you get here so fast?" Janai asked. "We drove."

"I flew," Nissa said. "It's easier."

"Flew?" Janai looked at Nissa. She was different now. Her hair was clean and flowing, her clothes were sparkly and Janai could see two translucent wings peeking out from behind. "But how ... and ... " Janai stood and stared at Nissa. "You don't look homeless anymore."

"Well, I am," she said. "I live on the streets. I wait until I meet someone with a wish that grows from deep within their heart. Then, I grant them that wish."

Janai looked around. She expected to see her aunt charging through the crowd to haul her back to the finish line. No one moved. In fact, there were no sounds at all. There were no cheers, no conversations, no wind, no bird songs. No one moved. She looked at Nissa.

"What did you do?"

"Oh, I didn't do anything," she said with a smile. "You did."

"Me?"

"Yes, you. You made a wish, well three of them, and now we have to decide which wish you want."

"We?"

"Yes, and we must do it soon before Durack gets here," the fairy paused. "He can't fly as fast as I can. He hates it when I get to a wish first."

"Oh, okay," Janai said. Although nothing felt okay. "Are you my fairy godmother?"

Nissa let out a laugh. "Oh goodness no! We stopped that years ago. There are too many of you and not enough of us. Durack and I disguise ourselves as homeless people and wait until someone worthy of receiving a wish comes along. Like you. You were polite."

"So, I don't get all three wishes?"

"Goodness no, just pick one and we'll be on our way." Nissa spread out her translucent wings and smiled at Janai. "I believe you wanted to be super tall?"

"Wait just one darn minute!" a gruff voice called from behind the tree. "She had other wishes. You're not the only wish granter here Nissa." Durack stood beside Nissa and glared at Janai. "You also wished your parents would stop running and you wanted them to stay home. I can grant you one of those wishes."

Janai looked back and forth between the two. They were all good wishes. Durack, now without the foul-smelling breath and dirt-caked clothes, didn't look so bad. Aside from the dark brown wings, he looked pretty normal, like a kind grandpa.

"Choose wisely, Janai," Nissa cautioned. "You've always wanted to be taller. If you were tall you could run marathons like your parents and you'd be able to spend more time with them. The kids wouldn't tease you at school for being short. No more being called a baby and short stop."

"Or ..." Durack pushed Nissa aside and crouched down to Janai's level. "You could have parents that didn't run marathons, or parents that stayed home with you, all the time. You'd like that, wouldn't you?"

"Ummmm, yeah, I would." Janai glanced over her shoulder to the crowd behind her. They were still frozen in time. She hated crowds. She hated being unseen, unheard, and unimportant. "Yeah, yeah, I want them to be home all the time with me."

Durack smiled showing pointed teeth. "Excellent," he hissed. Janai's stomach lurched and then they were in her bedroom. "Your wish is my command." Durack bowed and disappeared. Nissa was nowhere to be seen.

Janai called out. "Mom? Dad?"

"What!" came the sharp response. Janai followed the voice into the living room. The TV was on and the coffee table was littered with beer and pop cans, candy wrappers, chip bags and take-out containers. Her mother and father sat at opposite ends of the couch in their pajamas. Their hair was tangled and greasy. Their eyes were glazed over. They looked like they never left the house.

Her father glared at her. "I said, what! Are you deaf as well as stupid? Make yourself useful. Go to the store and get us some chocolate bars." He tossed his ATM card at her and turned back to the TV. Her mother never looked at her.

Janai picked up the bank card and ran back to her room. These weren't her parents. Her parents were never mean to her. They ate healthy and the house was usually tidy. Sure, they spent a lot of time travelling, but they always took her with them. She pulled herself up on her bed. This wasn't right.

"I don't want this wish," she sobbed. She heard a popping sound and Durack stood in front of her.

"You don't like my gift?" he said, sarcasm dripping from his lips.

"No, no I don't!" Janai hopped off the bed. "Those aren't my parents! My parents love me, and they take care of me and they take me places. I want my parents back!" she shouted.

"Calm down," Durack said. "It was kind of a double wish, I can give you the other one instead, but no more take backs."

"Just do it!" Janai hollered. "I want my mom and dad back!"

Durack laughed. "Okay, okay."

Janai's stomach lurched again. Durack was gone. Maybe things had changed for the better. She quickly made her way down the hall. "Mom? Dad?" she called.

"In the kitchen, honey." It was her mom. She ran into the kitchen to see both her parents sitting at the table doing a puzzle. Something wasn't right. The chairs had wheels.

"Come help us, kiddo," her father said. He pushed back from the table and patted his lap.

This wasn't right. Not only could her parents not run marathons anymore, they also couldn't walk! She went over to her dad and let him lift her up.

"Nissa, can you bring us some tea please?"

"Nissa? What is she doing here?" Janai turned to see the fairy in the kitchen wearing an apron and holding a fresh pot of tea.

"I live here silly girl," the very non-fairy looking fairy said. "Thanks to you I now have a home."

Janai looked puzzled and hopped down off her dad's lap.

This wasn't right either. "Can you help me with something in my room, Nissa?" She ran to her bedroom and waited for Nissa to join her.

"I told you to be careful, didn't I?" the fairy said as she closed the bedroom door.

"What happened?" Janai asked.

"There was an accident at the race," Nissa said. "A car plowed through the runners. Your parents were injured. I had just given you back your green pencil. Remember? Your parents were hurt, your aunt was hysterical, there were police and ambulance everywhere. We went to the homeless shelter for a few hours. I got cleaned up, you got some food and then we walked to the hospital. Your parents were so thankful, they hired me to look after all of you. Remember?"

Janai blinked. "I kind of remember. The homeless shelter was nice. I remember talking to one of the ladies. Was she a fairy, too?"

"No dear, she was a person. Not all homeless people are fairies. Sometimes they are just people who need our help."

Janai rubbed her eyes. "Wait a minute! That's not what happened. Durack did this. He said no take backs, but I want my other wish instead. I want to be tall!"

"I believe you said, super tall." Nissa winked and Janai felt a familiar lurch in her stomach. She blinked and Nissa was gone. So was her bed. In its place was a king size bed that took up most of the room.

"Breakfast is ready," her mother called from the kitchen. "Hurry up, you don't want to be late for school." Janai rushed down the hallway. Her chair was much larger before, but it fit her perfectly. She was tall! No, super tall! She wolfed down her breakfast and ran all the way to school. When she got there, things took a turn for the worse.

"Hey, how's the weather up there?" It was one of her classmates, the one who called her short stop.

"Yo, stretch, the Harlem Globetrotters called, they want you to join them!" hollered another.

She stepped into her classroom and heard two girls whispering as she walked by. "I bet her parents were giraffes."

Janai hung her head. The kids that were mean to her when she was super short, were just as mean when she was super tall. None of her wishes were any good. She wished she'd never wished them at all.

The room faded away and Janai found herself back in the park. This time there were three fairies.

"Hello Janai, I'm Titania. I hope these two didn't cause you too much grief." Janai blinked. Titania placed her hand on the back of Nissa's neck and another on Durack's. "Get out of here," she scolded and the two disappeared. Janai blinked twice. Titania was still there.

"Those two really need to find a better hobby." Titania

sat down and patted the ground beside her. "Come, sit." Janai did as she was told.

"Are you my fairy godmother?" she asked.

Titania laughed. "No dear, I am the Queen of the Fairies and I'm here to stop those two idiots from ruining your life."

"Are you an evil queen?" Janai gulped.

"No dear, I'm just a ruler who tries to keep her kind in line. We appear when good people need to learn a lesson, or when they are struggling in their life. Those two tend to take it a bit too far. As for you, I think it's time you got back to your aunt." Titania waved her hand and the scene before them sprang back to life. People cheered as the runners completed the home stretch of the marathon.

"My parents are okay? I'm not super tall?"

"Everything is the same as it was," the fairy queen said. "Take my advice, let your parents know you want more time with them. Talk to someone about the bullying. It's easy to wish for change. It takes courage to make the change."

Janai nodded and ran back to her aunt just in time to see her parents cross the finish line. They made their way over to Janai and lifted her up between them and gave her a big, sweaty hug.

Maybe, just maybe, they could live happily ever after.

Read My Shorts

Fore for Four!

"Creating a portal to a tenth hole was ingenious!" Major Hadler said as he happily snapped his tail pincers together.

"Thank you, Major." General Gardor pressed a button and leaned into his microphone.

"Camouflage holograms in place?"

"Yes, sir!" came the reply. "Looks like a fairway lined with trees."

"Turf tarp secured over the trap?"

"Yes, sir," another voice called out. "Looks like a putting green."

"Controlled navigation ball on tee?"

"Check," a third voice shouted.

"Glass cage in place?"

"Aye sir!" acknowledged a fourth voice.

General Gardor looked at his readouts. "High alert. Prey nearing the portal. Activate now!" He watched his screen with anticipation. There was a slight pop as a lone golfer drove his cart through the portal. He looked confused, but happy with this discovery. He picked out a club and walked to the tee box. He saw a ball already in place, looked around, shrugged, then steadied his stance and swung. Much to his surprise the ball flew true and landed on the green.

"Steady, steady, everyone," Gardor whispered into the mic. A minute later, the golfer stepped on the green and the turf collapsed, sending him plummeting downward. "Activate transporter!" Gardor shouted and seconds later a glass cage appeared before him with the golfer inside. "Major Hadler, let Chef know we have our appetizer."

Gardor pressed the mic button again. "All right everyone, reset and look sharp. Three more and we've got ourselves a feast!"

The Secret Hallway

Janice sulked as she watched a tour guide lead a dozen people into the library. She hated strangers wandering through what was once her home. She decided to follow them.

"This is Dash Roughhew's library where he once seduced a multitude of rising stars." The tour guide ushered the group into the room. "He had a strong reputation as a womanizer." Janice snuck into the room and watched as the guide pressed a dowel on the side of a bookcase. A secret door opened onto a hallway.

The guide stepped in and everyone followed, including Janice. The hallway was narrow and smelled like old books, cigars, and mice droppings.

The guide turned on her flashlight and continued. "The police believe his new bride locked him in here, hoping to cure him of his philandering ways. Unfortunately, she was killed by a burglar the same night Roughhew disappeared. Roughhew died a slow death within these soundproofed walls. He was discovered a year later during renovations."

The group turned left, towards the main bedchamber. Janice felt a hand grip hers and pull her to the right.

"What took you so long?" a voice whispered in her ear. "Let's get out of here." A bright light appeared at the end of the hallway. Janice tried to pull away.

"Go where?" she asked as the realization hit her. "Dash?"

"Yes, my bride, of course it's me. Let's go."

She held his hand as they stepped into the light, together.

Grandpa's Other Name

"Grandpa!" Tommy said, as he rushed into the room. "Do you have another name? Other than Grandpa, I mean."

The old man smiled. "It's Frank, lad. Grandpa's a title, but it's a special one."

"Oh, okay." Tommy didn't looked convinced. "Grandpa, my friend Danny said that his dad said that his dad ..." Tommy paused, making sure his words had lined up without falling over. He nodded in agreement with himself and continued. "anyway he said he knew you when you were at school. His name was weird too, like Woody or something." Tommy looked up at his Grandpa.

"At school you say? I don't remember going to school with anyone named Woody."

"No ... no, not school, somewhere else. I don't remember now, but he said everyone there called you Shiv, and I said that was a funny kind of name, and he said it was a sort of knife, and that you ..."

"Well," Grandpa said, as he ruffled Tommy's hair, "that's the trouble with little boys, they've got dirt and marbles and comic books where their brains ought to be. Pay no mind to silly names, lad. I'm Grandpa Frank and that's all you need to know." Grandpa Frank stood up and headed towards the door.

"Where you going Grandpa?" Tommy asked.

"Well, I think it's too nice a day to spend cooped up indoors, so why don't we head on outside? You can take your new bike and show old Grandpa how well you can ride it. And while we're out, you can show me where this Danny lives."

About the Author

Darcy Nybo is an award winning author, freelance writer and journalist, as well as a writing instructor, writing coach, and hybrid publisher. When she's not glued to her keyboard, you'll find her outside in her garden, walking on the beach, or spending time with her two-legged and four-legged friends.

She has one other book of short stories, and three children's books completed, all available on Amazon. She is currently working on her second novel. The first one is still in the drawer and may be resurrected some day.

Books by Darcy Nybo

Read My Shorts: a short story collection.

Okanagan Tall Tales: an Okanagan short story collection.

Emma Jean Finds a Friend: A children's book written from the imaginary friend's perspective. Ages 5–9.

Bark! Swat! Crunch!: A children's picture book about what happens when two four-legged friends get bored when they are home alone. Ages 2–7.

The Great Grape Adventure: An activity book great for kids 6+, especially when touring in the Okanagan.

Manufactured by Amazon.ca
Bolton, ON